JESSIE'S SONG
and Other Stories

A RICHARD KASAK BOOK

JESSIE'S SONG
and Other Stories

CHEA VILLANUEVA

"In the Shadows of Love" previously appeared in *The Persistent Desire, a Femme-Butch Reader,* edited by Joan Nestle. Boston: Alyson Publications, 1992. Permission granted by the author.

"The Prom Queen" previously appeared in *The Body of Love*, edited by Tee A. Corinne. Austin, Texas: Banned Books, 1993. Permission granted by the author.

"Philly Gumbo" previously appeared in *Common Lives/Lesbian Lives*, number Twenty-seven. Iowa City, IA: 1988.

"Friends" previously appeared in *Riding Desire*, edited by Tee A. Corinne. Austin, Texas: Banned Books, 1991. Permission granted by the author.

"The Dozens" previously appeared in *Outrage*, edited by Mona OIkawa, Dionne Falconer, Rosamund Elwin, Ann Decter. Canada: Women's Press, 1993. Permission granted by the author.

"Girlfriends" by Chea Villanueva, 1987. Permission granted by the author.

Jessie's Song and Other Stories
Copyright © 1995 Chea Villanueva

First Richard Kasak Book Edition 1995

First Printing March 1995

ISBN 1-56333-235-3

Cover Art © Brian Lynch
Cover Design by Kurt Griffith

Manufactured in the United States of America
Published by Masquerade Books, Inc.
801 Second Avenue
New York, N.Y. 10017

Dedicated to my sister
Margaret Lorenz
for all her love and encouragement,
and my father Jerome
for giving me the strength to tough it out
in a homophobic world.

JESSIE'S SONG
and Other Stories

IN *the* SHADOWS *of* LOVE

Six: 1958

I am six years old when I knock on your door. Your mother answers.

"Can Dale come out to play?" I am breathless. My heart pounds through the white T-shirt covering my thin chest.

Your mother nods. "All right, but don't go too far."

I grab your hand without hesitation. You run with me knowingly. Knowing we will play "the game" today.

"Is your sister home? Is her boyfriend with her?" You squeeze my hand.

We climb the fence in the back of the house I share with my parents and older sister. The venetian blinds covering the window are slightly open. My sister is making out on the couch with her boyfriend, Tony.

Dale and I take turns peeking. "Shh," I say. I take her

hand and pull her to the ground. "Let's play that I'm Tony and you're Sissy."

She pulls away. "But why can't I be Tony and you be Sissy? Why do I always have to be the girl?"

"Because I said so. I'm never gonna be a girl!" My feelings are hurt and I run. Dale chases me and I am happy. I stop running.

"C'mon," I say, "let's go back and watch them kissin' and then I'll kiss you, too."

We kissed all afternoon on the back steps in the yard. The afternoon sun was setting. My sister straightened her dress. Her boyfriend stood up reluctantly. My father would be home soon.

"Dale!" It was time for Dale to be going, too. "My mother's calling me."

I stood up and jammed my hands in the pockets of my jeans, reluctantly, mimicking Tony. "Well, I guess I'll see ya tomorrow and we can kiss again."

I took a cigar band out of my pocket along with a penknife, a lucky penny, and some baseball cards. "Here, Dale, let's pretend we're married." I slid the cigar band ring over her finger. "But don't forget, I'm gonna be the husband and you're gonna be the wife."

"Dale!" Dale's mother was calling again.

"OK, Tony, I'll see ya tomorrow," Dale said and smiled. A new game had started....

Ten: 1962

I am ten years old and my mother is dead. I am alone in the house that I share with my father. He's left for his night job at the factory and I am left alone. I dial your number. You answer.

"Did he leave?"

"Yeah. Can you sneak out?"

I make myself ready for Dale. I comb my hair back with water, put on a clean undershirt.

Dale is here in a few minutes. I hear her whistle, hear her coming in through the back door. She's crying. "They're fighting again! I hate it when they fight!"

I put my arms around her. "Dale, did you eat yet? My father left me some food."

We eat with the venetian blinds turned down and the radio turned low. We know we have to hide what we have no name for. Dale washes the dishes. I watch her with a warm glow spreading up my thighs.

"C'mon, Dale, let's lay on the couch."

The couch is narrow. I lie on top of her. I unbutton her blouse. She pulls the shirt over my head. We lay still. Chest to chest, lips to lips.

"Dale, I want to do something different. Let's take our pants off this time."

There is no hesitation, and within a few moments two pairs of jeans are on the floor.

"Now take off your underpants."

She hesitates with this new order. "But what if your father comes home?"

"Don't worry about it, I put the chain on the door."

She slides her underpants down. I am back on top of her. We are naked. Chest to chest, lips to lips, bare pubis to pubis. I grind into her. Force her to ride with me. This new thing feels good, but I wonder if there is something more....

till after the night. Her parents fight more and
I slip my hands in her blouse her breasts are so
much bigger I squeeze them from the puts nails
she digs me she that I've more well doesn't want her
for the night. Diana Ross and the Supremes tears and
whisper me she to I know how to her tonight tears.

Thirteen: 1965

Today I am thirteen. Dale is here. She is staying over again. Her parents fight more on the weekends. It is night. The lights are out except for the single glow from the television set. We are watching the TV with my father. He falls asleep in his chair. Dale and I are on the couch and I slip my hands in her blouse. Her breasts are so much bigger than mine. Mine are two small bumps, but Dale doesn't mind. I squeeze them with both hands. I feel her sweat running from her armpits. I pinch her nipples. She digs her nails into my hands, pulls my hands from her breasts. "This feels good," she breathes. From the TV Diana Ross and the Supremes are singing, "Whisper you love me, boy...you know how to talk to me, baby..."

I feel a familiar wetness between my legs, and I tug at the elastic waistband of her shorts. I slide my hand down lower till I touch the fabric of her panties. My hand enters and I slip my probing finger into her groove. My wetness spreads. Deeper. I join hers. She joins mine. Deeper. My father stirs from his chair. We move apart fast. He reaches for the light. Faster. Dale pulls up her waistband and smooths out her shorts. I wipe her wetness on my jeans.

Sixteen: 1968

We are sixteen. Dale and I. We are lying in my bed. My father is at work. Her parents are fighting again. On these nights she sleeps with me.

She is naked. Her long ebony hair hides her breasts. I brush the hair away with my lips and begin the night's ritual. But tonight is different. I have never tasted a woman and so this night will be special. She bites my neck, my ears, and comes in my mouth.

I am dreaming I have a penis. I put it deep inside of her and imagine we are making a baby....

She is crying, "It hurts," and I slip my fingers from her vagina. She takes my hand and places it on her naked belly. My fingers are bloody from probing too far. She has given me her virginity.

I lick the blood from my fingers.

Seventeen: 1969

Today I am seventeen. A runaway from reform school.

Short hair slicked back into a DA with a little help from Olivo, Kings Men after-shave, white shirt open at the collar, black V-neck bad boy sweater, jeans, and penny loafers.

I wait at the gate of St. Dominic's for Dale. I am sentimental. I hum, "Ain't no mountain high enough, ain't no valley low enough, ain't no river wide enough to keep me from gettin' to you, babe..."

The bell rings, signaling the end of the school day, and pretty girls in navy uniforms step lively out the door. I lean against the wall of the schoolyard, hands in pockets, and a cigarette dangling from the corner of my lips. Pretty girls glance shyly at the pretty delinquent boy and I look back boldly. The pretty girls blush.

Dale! She sees me, but waits till the yard is clear from

prying eyes. No one must know. I see a nun that taught me in the sixth grade and I lower my face.

A worldly black man saunters by. "Bulldagger! Ain't nothin' but a bulldagger!"

The nun looks. My heart thumps, there's a lump in my throat, I remember the song, "...ain't no mountain high enough..." The nun walks on. All she sees is a young boy.

Dale is coming toward me. One more step and she walks out the gate. Dale! I take her arm and we walk far from the school, far from the world, far from worldly black men. We enter an alley. We need no words. I lean her against a wall, I put my leg between hers, she drops her books, we kiss long and hard.

A man enters the alley to pee. We break away. I look for a bottle to break over his head. Ready to protect my girl, ready to fight for my butchness. But all he sees in his wine stupor is a boy and a girl. The man zips up his pants, embarrassed, and leaves. He was young once.

Dale cried, "I never thought I'd see you again." I cry with her.

Too soon we both know this moment can't last. Too soon the cops will be looking for me, too soon we'll have no place to go. I don't want to make love in an alley, don't want to limit our love to the street.

"Baby," I say, "I just had to see you. I gotta go now, but just promise you'll wait for me."

Dale promised and whispered all her love forever with her mouth and tongue and hands....

Eighteen: 1970

I am eighteen years old. Home from reform school, I am
fighting with my family. My sister wants me to look like a
girl. My father wants me to get a job. My brother-in-law
doesn't want me in his house. No one understands me.
No one but Dale.

Funny, but I hadn't seen much of Dale since the first
night we spent together after my release from reform school.
Everything was like old times then. Dale met me at the bus
terminal. We bought popcorn and smoked cigarettes in the
back of the bus that would take me home—and back to the
comfort of Dale's arms. She was still wearing the gold friendship ring I had given her at sixteen.

But as I said, something had changed since the night
we made love in my father's yard. We had a couple of beers
that night and I wanted her badly. Badly enough to tear her

blouse and reckless enough not to care who caught us. She wanted me, too, wanted me enough to spread her legs under the light of the moon. We were both naked from the waist down when my next-door neighbor caught us. There I was on top of Dale, and there was Dale moaning "...do it harder baby..."

All at once a flash of light brought us back from the brink of another climax.

Something changed when the talk started and my family started to pressure me to go out with boys.

Dale was never at home when I called and she was suddenly too busy to come out and walk with me. I no longer heard the familiar whistle outside my bedroom window after my dad left for work. I slept for weeks in our love sheets, smelling her scent, rubbing my face in it, listening to Carole King singing, "tonight you're mine completely, you give your love so sweetly... Will you still love me tomorrow..."

I found out soon enough that she was seeing this guy Sammy. It broke my heart, but I still had to see her. She had to choose between us. It was going to be either Sammy or me. She could not have us both. I wanted her to choose me. If she wanted a man I would be her man.

I slicked my hair back, put the switchblade in the back pocket of my chinos, and zipped up my black leather jacket. I wanted her badly enough to put up a fight.

I found her and Sammy parked in a car near her house. They were in the front seat. He had his hand on her leg. She had her lips on his mouth. I was sick with jealousy and tried to break the rolled-up windows with my fist. My hands were bleeding when Sammy got out of the car.

"What's the matter, butch? You lose your girlfriend or somethin'?" Sammy laughed and came toward me swinging a baseball bat. "Look, bitch, I want you to stay away from my girlfriend or I'll mess you up bad. She doesn't want to see you anymore!" Sammy spat. "Everybody in this neighborhood knows you're a fuckin' dyke."

Dale came between us as I closed in on Sammy with my knife. I would kill the bastard! I wasn't afraid of him or his bat.

Dale's scream tore through my heart, ripped out my guts, and left me lying on a cold street. "Stop! Just stop! Leave him alone and leave me alone. I don't want you anymore! Things are different now."

She cried and tried to hug me. I ran away.

I didn't want them to see my tears.

Eighteen: a few months later

Today I woke up in the hospital.

Drugged enough to hide the pain, but alert enough not to kill the memory....

I walked in front of a car last night. My intentions were good. I was eighteen, my girlfriend left me, and I wanted to die.

I remember the sirens and the ambulance racing to deliver my broken body to the emergency ward. Remember the surgeon's words to my father.

"Ruptured spleen, lacerated liver, internal bleeding..."

I remember my family gathered around the gurney, and the words of the priest administering extreme unction (the Catholic prayers before dying).

I was spaceless enough to let my body slip into the dark tunnel to the other side of life, but angry enough to remember how I got there.

Dale was standing with my sister, holding my hand, her tears spilling onto my face. I was angry enough to remember Dale with Sammy. Sammy with Dale.

Bitter words turning over in my mind. Dale with Sammy...

The prayers before dying.

I am eighteen years old, and suddenly I don't want to die.

Nineteen: 1971

Today I am nineteen.

I saw Dale today.

I was on a bus on my way to nowhere when I saw her.

The bus stops. I get off. The year-old scar across my abdomen aches with the memory of a love that never said good-bye.

Dale! She turns and bends to soothe the crying child. A baby boy, born from Sammy.

"Dale, are you happy?"

"Yes." She answers without meeting my eyes. Suddenly she looks older, tired, and not happy at all.

I remember the days of lying in each other's arms and I-love-you-forevers....

At once I feel release from this tired woman with baby, and I realize that the Dale I knew was gone and would never be again.

"How are you?" she asks, finally finding the courage to meet my gaze. "Are you happy?"

I hesitate, remembering the contours of her body, her smell, her taste, and the feeling of my fingers in her folds.

I tell her about my new love, job, and my new life.

She tells me he's left her.

We stay in the present and talk until the next bus arrives that will take us away from our past.

Finally it's good-bye.

I board the bus and never see her again.

The LETTER

December 1993

Dear Susan,

    I'm sitting here listening to Major Harris singing "Love Won't Let Me Wait." It took me back in time, slow dancing with you at Barone's Variety Room, the bar in the back alley on Quince Street. It made me remember how you felt in my arms. So light, so mine, how we fit together...

1973—Has it been that long? It's been twenty years since I walked into that Women's Center in West Philadelphia. I didn't want to go, but friends prompted me. It wasn't my style. I needed the bars that night.

Flashback—You sitting, legs crossed, talking with other women. You were the only femme in a circle of women too into their politics to admit their attraction to you.

And me—the only butch, too sure I knew I wanted you.

You looked at me once, as only a femme can when she's hungry for only one kind of loving. I felt the electricity, smelled your perfume, knew I'd leave with you that night with the sureness that I loved you, that it would last a lifetime, that you loved me too....

1993—I'm sitting in a bar watching women I don't care about. Women who are so into their androgyny that they view me as a threat to their existence, banishing me to the door with their comments. "Is that a man or a woman?"

Flashback 1974—I bought a new suit today, had my hair cut, and wore your favorite cologne. I surprised you by coming home early with a dozen red roses and a new dress for my baby.

You were in the bathtub, soaking in candlelight and my favorite perfume. You pulled me into the water with you. Me with my dirty end-of-the-week workclothes and printer's ink.

We never made it out to the club that night. After our bath, we dressed for each other, drank champagne, and made love in every corner of our apartment....

Has it been that long since I walked you to your car, and our lips met for the first time, not wanting to let go, not wanting to admit we were in love already?

1993—I'm still thinking of you. Looking at old photographs of a young butch and her proud femme.

I bought you wildflowers and ice cream that day in the park. You held my arm and defied society's rules by insisting we get our picture taken in all our glory of us together....

I remember Friday nights, getting all dressed up. You getting your hair done and filing those nails to a fine red point, knowing later they'd mark my back for keeping you up all night...

Remember the rush when we'd walk into the club, everybody's eyes on us? The perfect couple—the beautiful femme and the handsome young butch. Was it that long ago when I was twenty and you were thirty?

We had respect in those days. The feminists stayed in the coffeehouses, while we ruled the bars in our suits and dresses, slicked-back hair, heels and stockings. Who ever thought it would end?

Flashback 1975—I remember you holding me against your breast as only a lover can do. Telling me you were dying. The endless trips to faith healers, doctors, and the strength in our love couldn't keep you with me just a little while longer....

Has it been that long since the night you were tired, and insisted I go play cards with our two best friends? Has it?

I remember the taste of your lipstick when I kissed you for the last time. Remember playing cards with an uneasy feeling that my life was changing, that the life I had known would cease to exist and be banished to memory.

1993—Has it been that long that love was innocent, when you took off my tie and hung my suitcoat so carefully on a hanger, when you came to me smelling of jasmine and dressed in lace and satin?

It's been so long since someone cared to smooth my hair back, tell me I was handsome, tell me they were mine....

I fear I can't love anymore, fear I'm out of time. Does love like ours exist anymore?

Flashback 1975—Such an eerie feeling when I walked into our apartment. I knew when I put the key in the door that you were so gone out of this life that I'd search forever and never find you....

Reading your letter afterward with the knowledge that the tumor had grown and was causing you pain I could never heal. You loved me enough to send me away so I couldn't undo the rope that snapped your neck. Loved me enough to tell me one more time that you loved me...

1993—Has it been eighteen years since I stood crying in the rain, cursing the earth that swallowed you up?

Has it been that long since I slipped the gold band on your finger and exchanged vows in that church on Chestnut Street?

I still look the same. Maybe a few lines from a life filled with hardness. Same haircut, suit, tie, same cocky assertiveness when I walk into a bar, same hungry eyes when I look at a femme.

People like us are so few now—it doesn't happen often, but our youth lingers on in memories of smoke-filled rooms and jukeboxes....

The BUS RIDE

The year I was sixteen I dropped out of school and got my first job, working in a candle factory. I had to be at work by 6:30 in the morning, so I got up at 5:00 every day and rode a bus for forty-five minutes.

It was a cold winter that year, ten degrees below zero. I dressed in layers of clothing. Long underwear over my jockey shorts and undershirt, two pairs of thermal socks, two sweatshirts, two pairs of gloves, combat boots, and leather jacket.

The ladies who worked as domestic help always thought I was a little man, but the nurses knew different.

This one morning I met this nurse.

I was sitting in the back of the bus minding my own business and trying to keep awake by smoking a cigarette, when this really attractive nurse about twenty years old asks me if she can have a smoke. The next thing I know, she asks me if I'm gay and do I have a girlfriend. Well, I had a girlfriend that was my steady, and I told her that, but she kept talking to me anyway. I took a long hard look at her and thought, "Why's she wanna know all these things about me?" We kept talking through a couple of bus stops (mostly it was her asking me questions).

The next thing I knew, she was telling me I was really cute and then she puts her hand on my leg and starts to rubbing it like she was gonna put her hand in my crotch. And me, I was trying to look cool like I always do; like this kind of thing happens to me every day. I could tell she was getting hot 'cause then she wants to give me her phone number. This chick had her own apartment and a car, and would I mind coming over some time.

To be honest, she was really coming on to me and she was really pretty in a slutty kind of a way. For a quick minute I thought about fucking her, and then thought about my girlfriend (who I was really in love with). So I told this chick "no way." I never even slept with another girl besides my girlfriend, and this nurse was a lot older than me.

Well, she kept playing with my leg until we got to my stop, and I said it was nice talking to you, I gotta go now.

I saw her a few more times on the bus after that, but she always ignored me and tried to look the other way. But I could tell she was looking. It was just as well, 'cause me and my girl was gonna get married anyway.

The PROM QUEEN

Toy and Rocky were going to the prom!

Toy wore a green chiffon dress over a black slip, black bra, garters, and stockings. Her teased hair was held together with Aquanet hair spray and My Sin perfume.

Rocky, on the other hand, wore a baby blue tuxedo, starched white shirt with topaz cufflinks, and hair slicked back with Olivo, smelling like an AquaVelva commercial. Rocky had spent all day pomading her black hair to a gloss, and Toy spent all afternoon padding her bra to a 36-C.

After the prom they planned to make out in Rocky's blue '66 Malibu.

They had been doing this every night for a year, but tonight would be special because of the prom.

Toy and Rocky walked in hand in hand. Of course, they were the only girl couple there. Some of the girlfriends stopped to admire Toy's corsage and scan to see who her prom date was. When they saw her holding Rocky's arm they did a double take. It was no mistake. There was Rocky trying to look cool and trying to look like a boy for all the world to see.

Who did she think she was, anyway? Everybody knew Rocky Corvair from last year. She was the girl always getting suspended and the only girl to drop out of St. Maria Goretti High School in 1967.

The girlfriends mumbled, "Nice dress, Toy," and ran to grab their dates. Behind Toy's back they whispered.

"The nerve of her ruining our prom by bringing that Rocky Corvair. A girl! Can you imagine? How did Rocky think she could just walk in here and we wouldn't notice her? And Toy, did you see that dress she was wearing? She looked like a slut with those black stockings, and you could see she had on black underwear underneath that dress. I always knew she had a bad reputation."

The crowd hushed when they saw Sister Alice and Mother Superior heading across the gym.

They were over by the punch bowl when Mother Superior grabbed Rocky by the ear, took Toy by the arm, spilling her punch over her 36-C, and escorted them out the door. She would be contacting their parents and would deal with Toy directly first thing Monday morning!

Poor Toy and Rocky. They had dressed their finest and now they had to leave. Toy was visibly upset. Not only did she have punch juice on her new dress, but now the tears were spilling over onto her new chest and the foam was coming out of her bra.

All Rocky could think about was getting her into the backseat of her Malibu.

"C'mon, Toy, you look fine. You were the best-dressed girl there, and I love you for it."

All Toy could think about was getting suspended from school. This was her senior year and she looked forward to graduation, marrying Rocky, and going to the beauty academy.

Rocky took out a handkerchief to wipe the tears. This made Toy cry even more. Rocky jammed her hands into her pockets. She felt helpless and looked it.

"What'd I do now?"

"Baby, you're ruining my mascara."

Rocky pleaded. "Well, look, I'm sorry. It's not my fault they didn't want us there. Look, Toy, don't let them ruin our good time. I got some money and gas in the car. We can drive down the shore and get a hotel room. If you don't want to stay out all night we can park somewhere and dance to our own music."

Toy was sorry. Rocky was being so sweet, and she did want to be with her. And Rocky was right. She really was the best dressed girl at the prom, and Rocky definitely looked better than the dates those pompous bitches came with.

That night Rocky and Toy ended up parking at the edge of the riverbank.

Rocky's new expertise was unhooking Toy's bra with one hand while the other massaged Toy's thigh. Toy contented herself by watching Rocky's hand climb higher and higher until it reached her panties, which were clinging to her by her own dampness. By the time Rocky had her hand inside, Toy was chewing furiously on her Doublemint gum, and as she climaxed she bit Rocky's neck, leaving a trail of Doublemint from the nape of her neck to her shirt collar.

"Oh my god, oh my god!" Toy was crying as she came.

Rocky thought Toy had never had it so good, and continued to slip her fingers in and out of her lover's juicy pussy.

What Rocky didn't know was that Toy was exclaiming over her gum, which was now lost in Rocky's hair.

It was a memorable night for both of them.

PHILLY *Gumbo*

My best memories about Philadelphia was Sassy.

Beautiful Sassy Rios, with the steaming cup of coffee in the morning, and the hand-on-the-hip grin that seemed to make things better no matter how evil your day was.

The TV commercials say, "Things go better with Coke..." But they lied.

Things go better with Sassy....

You see, I was hangin' out with her best femme friend, Toni, but Toni all of a sudden decided she wanted to be a butch and sometimes we'd get our roles mixed up. Like me always getting on top and refusing to wear that pink nightgown.

I'd tell her, "Toni, don't be askin' me to put on that stupid-ass pink thing. You wear it if you like it so much!" And Toni would roll over, put the blanket over her head, and wish she could die.

I mean, can you imagine Toni Tucker the way she looks

now, with her short Gerri curls slicked back and black leather jacket and starched white shirt complete with cufflinks and gray wool pants with the cuffs turned up and black wing-tip shoes wearing a pink nightgown? I swear, if Toni was a dude she'd look like Cool Breeze, the pimp who we knew from the Wayne Ave. Lounge.

Cool Breeze was all right, though. He was always taking us for rides in his white Rolls-Royce, or letting me drive it around the block to impress the new babe I'd be cruising.

Yeah, for a pimp, I guess Cool Breeze was OK.

One night Toni and I got into one of our fights. I showed up at her place wearing the same kind of suit that she had on and I thought she would really die this time.

"What's the matter with you, Val? Take off that tie and act like you know."

"Fuck you, Toni. If you can wear one, so can I. If you don't like it I'll find somebody else to go out with!"

I started to walk out the door as Sassy started in. Toni grabbed my arm and I stayed, but only because I wanted to check out Sassy.

She was wearing a black spandex jumpsuit and leather high-heeled boots, standing with that hand-on-the-hip grin, with the brownest skin and eyes, and the blackest curly hair, looking six feet tall with those long slim legs, the kind you love to wrap around your neck; I knew I had to see her again if I had to wait forever....

So that's how I met Sassy.

I glanced at Toni looking all ridiculous in her suit and knew we were going to call it quits real soon. I kept my tie on and the three of us made it to the Swan Club. It was there that Toni met T.J. and I kissed Sassy in the bathroom.

She was hot as she rubbed her hand around my neck, up and down my spine, and put that snake tongue in my mouth. I just knew I wasn't going to be cold that night....

But Sassy had other plans, 'cause Toni was her best friend. It was cool to mess around in the bathroom at the Swan Club, but definitely not cool to wrap her legs around my neck in my bedroom.

I went home alone and stayed up all night thinking of ways to get Sassy into my bed.

A week went by before I saw Toni again, because T.J. was keeping her busy. One lonely night I ran into her at the Wayne Ave. Lounge. We were friends again, and played music from the jukebox and checked out the babes. Brandy and Maria came by, but I definitely wasn't interested and let them know it.

"What's the matter with you, Val?" Maria wanted to know.

"Oh, she's got a crush on Sassy."

"Sassy who?"

"You know Sassy."

"You mean tall Sassy?"

"Yeah, girl. Who else we know by Sassy?"

Maria looked like she wanted to slap my face, and stormed out the door, while Brandy quietly said, "Go 'head, girl."

Twenty minutes later Maria returned and whispered something to Toni, and Toni walked out without saying good-bye.

"What did you tell her, Maria?" I could sense something was going on that had to do with me.

"Sassy's outside."

"My Sassy?" I nearly fell off my chair.

"Her and Toni gotta talk about this. I thought you two were goin' together."

"Now, you know me and Toni ain't goin' together. We just messed around a few times, it's no big deal."

"That ain't what Toni been tellin' everybody."

"Look, she knows I sleep with other women, we're just

friends. And besides, she ain't even my type anymore."

Maria got mad all over again and walked back outside to see what was up, and Brandy bought me another drink.

"Don't let that chick work your nerves, she's just jealous 'cause she wants to go out with you. She's a little slut, anyway."

"Maria?"

"Yeah, Maria. She's nineteen years old and done slept with more women and more men than I ever did, and I'm thirty-seven."

"I didn't know she slept with dudes."

"Yeah, girl. She let ol' Cool Breeze fuck her."

"Cool Breeze the pimp?"

"Uh hum."

"Damn. Check her the fuck out...." I never finished the conversation.

My girl Sassy, along with Toni and Maria, came walking in the door. Sassy walked up to me and put her arms around my neck like we had known each other's intimacies forever.

Toni kind of snarled and said, "Don't look so worried, it's cool. Me and Sassy talked and you can go out with her if you want. But don't fuck her up, or I'll bust you upside your head."

"Yeah, like you own me, Toni."

Sassy stood there with that hand-on-the-hip grin, and I knew things were going to be fine.

We had a beer, then made it over to my place and didn't get out of bed for three days until Toni, Maria, T.J., and Brandy came banging on my window.

"Well, did you get enough pussy?"

"You two must have got married, 'cause we ain't seen you for days."

By this time my sweet baby had gotten out of bed and was making coffee, wearing a see-through shirt and red lacy panties.

"Check you out, Sassy. It looks like Valentino got herself a sexy little wife now."

"Don't come in here talkin' shit, Toni. You know I ain't ready to play no house games...."

"Hey, Sassy girl, chill out. You know I'm messin' with you. I just never saw you like this."

And then Maria spoke up with a sly look in her eyes. "Must be love."

"Must be, huh, Valentino?" And Sassy goes grinning that hand-on-the-hip way.

Love? I was petrified. I mean, I liked her a lot, but I only knew her for three days and besides, I wasn't going to be hanging around Philly for too much longer. I looked at her again and thought, *Maybe I could grow to love her....* I had been living alone for so long that it would be nice to have a lover to come home to. I tried to imagine what life would be like living with Sassy.

Our relationship/friendship got pretty tight after two months. We spent a lot of time discovering the joys of our bodies and minds.

It didn't matter to Sassy whether I stayed up half the night typing poetry on a borrowed typewriter, or editing poems I had written to previous lovers. It didn't matter when I took off for New York City every weekend and left her my apartment keys, the rabbit, and some spare change. It didn't matter who I slept with in New York City, Washington, D.C., or the whole state of New Jersey, 'cause when she was home, her baby only saw her. And besides, her girl was gonna make it....

I came home every Monday to flowers on the kitchen table, flowers in the bedroom, and the scent of Sassy's perfume all over my sheets.

We had an agreement not to see each other the first night I got into town. In case I had been with another woman, Sassy didn't want to know about it. The rest of the week was spent hanging out at Toni's and T.J.'s, the Wayne Lounge, the Swan Club on Wednesday, driving around in Cool Breeze's car, or in bed.

It didn't matter to Sassy when I lost my job and had to steal food from the basement I shared with my upstairs neighbor. I swear that dude must have owned the Shop-Rite, the way he used to stock the basement with cases of soup, tuna fish, Wheaties, instant coffee, and peanut butter. We'd get up in the morning after he left for his job and load up our shopping bags, then take off for Seymore Street like two hurricanes.

Toni and T.J would be getting out of bed, saying, "What did you do now, rob a grocery store?" And Sassy would do her famous hand-on-the-hip grin. My girl was so pretty when she'd do that.

And Toni would say, "Oh, shit! Let me get on back to bed. I didn't see ya'll this mornin'; if that white dude catches you, you're gonna go to jail."

Well, that's the risk you have to take sometimes. That man had so many cases of food I doubt if he ever missed any.

Take T.J., for instance. She takes a risk every day getting her money by turning tricks. Like she says, she's her own boss.

"Ain't wastin' no time sittin' in some jive-ass office bustin' my red fingernails on some IBM typewriter. No fuckin' way..."

T.J. works when she wants to work, and saves her money so she can buy one of those high-rise condos in Center City. Then she says she'll settle down.

One night we were so broke that she turned seven tricks in an hour, made three hundred and fifty dollars, and took off. She came back two hours later with half the Shop-Rite and the liquor store, and went right to work in the kitchen. Girl, T.J. could cook—in, and out, of bed....

I had to go on a street patrol with the Guardian Angels, but she made sure she packed me enough fried chicken to feed all my friends throughout the night.

My best friends from the Angels were Fly Girl, Tony, Chink, and Angel, and we always hung tight together.

It didn't matter to Sassy when I spent most of my free time on patrol or hanging out at our headquarters.

One night I was standing watch at the door when Fly Girl and Angel came running up the street yelling that Chink was hurt. A couple of white boys from South Street tried to carve out half his stomach. The other Angels heard this and they were out for blood. When you have Angels for friends nobody better mess with you. I knew our leader, Tony, would want it handled a different way, so I got everybody into formation. We'd settle the score later, but for now Chink's condition took priority. We had trained together at the old South Philly headquarters and became good buddies, so I owed it to my friend to get to the hospital right away.

Fifty-one Guardian Angels marched to Einstein Hospital that night, from North Philly to South Philly in a silent, angry vigil. The cops were waiting there along with reporters and television crews. Tony and Willy C. were there, too, along with half the Camden, New Jersey, chapter. The reporters didn't care whether Chink would die. All they wanted was for us to look "bad" and stare into the cameras that were clicking away.

"What the fuck...," Tony said. "We're no movie stars. Man gets knifed and all you people care about is gettin' your story and pictures for the front page and Action News."

The cops wanted to know what we're doing there and ordered us off the sidewalk, or they're going to bust us for "disorderly conduct."

At that point we all got into formation around Tony and stared real hard at the honky policeman wearing badge number 1007, then we marched up the steps into the hospital so quietly that our leather combat boots seemed to be stepping on air.

They had Chink in a room by then, and we took turns going in. Who was going to stop us? We had all the Guardian Angels there, plus Chink's old lady. The brother couldn't talk, but we sensed by the vibes, and the fact that we were all sending him our energy, that he was going to pull through this.

We left him with four Angels and chipped in enough money to send his woman home in a taxi.

When I got back to Sassy's she was asleep.

It was almost seven in the morning and I was so tired I couldn't get undressed, so I crawled into bed still wearing my uniform and combat boots. She turned over and started to undress me, but I said, "Not right now, babe." And I knew she understood.

It was so cold in her apartment that the broken water pipe in the bathroom had frozen and there was a large sheet of ice on the floor. She pulled a blanket over me and we curled up under it and my leather jacket.

We went through a lot in the months that followed. Like my best friend being found raped and murdered, Toni and T.J.'s breakup, and Maria's drug overdose.

By that time I was so heavy into the Angels that I was spending 99 percent of my time at headquarters, or riding the subway.

It didn't matter to Sassy if we stopped going to our favorite club on Wednesday and that if she wanted to see me it had to be on the subway. It didn't matter whether my entire social life was centered around the Angels and if she wanted to be with me she had to sit on a hard bench at headquarters and watch me work out, answer phones, type reports, and train new recruits. Her baby was gonna be somebody someday.... Her baby was a famous Guardian Angel and a writer.

What did matter to Sassy was the lack of sex and my lack of commitment to the relationship. I still lived alone and the other 1 percent of my time was spent writing. Her baby was gonna be somebody, someday, but Sassy wanted to be somebody, too...like my old lady.

Sassy dreamed of a house with a garden, of us sitting together at the kitchen table with enough food so we didn't have to steal from any white man, and a queen-size bed with me in it.

If her baby wanted to live in New York City and be a famous writer it was OK, but Sassy wanted a committed relationship. She wanted to hear me say how much I loved her, but I never said those words.

I liked her a lot, admired her style, her commitment, and Sassy was just so real.

But love? I was petrified.

I had been hurt by love so many times that there wasn't anything left. I had lived alone for two years, afraid of relationships and afraid of women. But Sassy made me smile and laugh, and it felt good just holding her. As much as I tried, I just couldn't fall in love, and I wanted to so bad.

We had gone through the winter and were drifting into spring when Jolanda Martinez started coming around. She took one look at my girl Sassy, and it was love at first sight.

She made a point of going to Sassy's every night and giving her little presents, telling me I should pay more attention to her before somebody snatched her up. Finally, Sassy started flirting with her, hoping I would get jealous. Instead, I thought I was in love with somebody I had no business falling in love with and Sassy started sleeping with Jolanda, who said she was the best lover she ever had.

The end came when my "love" didn't respond to my feelings, and I needed Sassy to talk to.

Sassy with the steaming cup of coffee in the morning and the hand-on-the-hip smile. Sassy who guessed all my thoughts, my struggles, admired my values, and her girl was gonna be somebody, someday...

Sassy, who I suddenly realized I loved.

But Jolanda had taken control of the situation and told her one of us had to go. Sassy, who dreamed of a house with a garden and a queen-size bed, picked Jolanda, who dreamed of the same things. Jolanda, who loved Sassy with her body and soul, and always let her know. Now Jolanda, she was sure of.

Yeah, I was gonna be somebody, someday....

So was Sassy, Jolanda, Toni, T.J., and all our crowd.

It was in the month of April that I saw her for the last time. She gave me a poem and a hug and told me to take care, 'cause her girl was gonna make it.

FRIENDS

It had been getting dark in the studio for a while. The canvases stacked in the corner were an indistinguishable sculpture. Toward the west side of the city you could still see the lavender and orange streaks of sunlight reflected through the windows. It had been a hot, oppressive day and was turning into an equally oppressive night. The heat was rising lazily off the street. Even though it was early evening, when most New Yorkers were usually heading for dinner and entertainment, no one was rushing on the street below. The old vendor man on the corner packed up his fruit and vegetables; kids on roller skates gave up the race. And still we sat.

We had known each other for a long time. I wasn't sure of how many years. She kept track of things like that. Long enough to cry together, laugh together, and dream together; which is enough to make any two people friends. The ice had melted in our wine coolers. Neither of us made a move to replenish the glasses. We had been still, watching the dusk for some time. The visit had seen many long periods of silence, but we had been friends long enough to enjoy each other's company without idle talk.

I broke the spell by turning on the light and rummaging through the refrigerator for dinner. Cold ham and potato salad was enough of a supper. It was too hot to eat anything else. As I put the food onto paper plates, Frankie made more coolers. In a few minutes we were sitting, picking at the food with disinterested fingers.

"Well, do you have any ideas on what we can do tonight?"

"Not really. I'd like to go someplace that has all new faces instead of the tired old ones we've been looking at all summer."

Frankie looked away from the table. "I know what you mean. I could use some fresh conversation instead of the same gossip that's been going around."

We finished eating and Frankie picked up the glasses and carried them to the sink. I let my mind run with the dishwater as I contemplated all of New York City. I knew I'd heard of someplace new, just last week.... Luz had mentioned it.

"I've got it! How 'bout the place that just opened at Seventh and B? I think it's called Peg's. Well, what do you think?"

Frankie shrugged her shoulders. "I don't know. Is there a huge cover charge? I wonder if they play good dance music? Wonder if any good butches hang out there?"

"Well, I heard they have one bar, a DJ, and a couple video screens. If Luz goes there, it can't be that bad."

"What are we waiting for! Let's hurry and get outta here! What should I wear? I gotta take a shower...." Frankie disappeared down the hall to the bathroom still talking. I didn't bother to answer her. What was I going to wear?

Did I want to pick anyone up? I decided on a pair of tight black jeans, black high-tops, and a new Fruit of the Loom white sleeveless undershirt. "Perfect," I said to the mirror, flexing my muscles. I looked really good.

Frankie had finished her shower, so I went into the bathroom to wash up. When I came out, she had lit a joint, had the stereo on, and was grinding and gyrating her body to Aretha Franklin.

I stood watching until Frankie became aware of my presence in the room. The blood rushed to my head when she asked, "Well, how do I look? Do you think I'll meet anyone tonight?"

"You look great," I growled. "Come on, let's get outta here!"

An hour later we got off the subway and were heading down Avenue B. Frankie was still unsure about her appearance. "You sure I look OK?"

"Don't worry about it, honey. Everybody's going to look at you and ask who's the hot number."

"Yeah, you're right. Shit, they ain't seen nothin' hot as us in a long time!" Frankie strutted down the block, teasing me.

"Yo! Frankie! This must be the place." PEG's glared from a neon sign over the top of a building that once was a gas station. We would have walked by if not for the sign proclaiming it. The outside appearance still looked like a service station, but with the windows painted black. We joined a trio of women who were standing outside. The three were watching the street and looked uncertain about going in.

"Come on," Frankie said. "No point in hanging around out here."

It was dark inside despite the flashing lights on the dance floor. The walls were covered with mirrors, the usual gimmick to make a small place look bigger. In this case it only made the ten people look like twenty, and the bartender look twice as bored. There was no place to sit but at the bar, so we settled into a corner, anxious to watch women for the evening.

Two hours and six drinks later, the place had filled up. Women that came in together were still standing in the same groups, talking among themselves. The single women were sitting alone at the bar or leaning against the wall, depending on whether they wanted to be watched, or were watching. Couples were dancing in their accustomed manner and only the very young singles (who barely looked out of their teens) were dancing with newly acquired friends.

Frankie and I mingled our fill. Weaving through the crowd, we said hello to old acquaintances and tried to pick out a few new faces. The bar was too new, the evening still too young, and the crowd too sober for any real partying to go on. I stopped watching the dancers and turned to Frankie. "I can't stand it. These women are boring. If they aren't boring, they're stuck-up. Let's either dance or go home, I can't take it."

Frankie got up from the bar stool. "Let's dance then. I didn't get dressed to sit all night."

I danced with my eyes closed for the first few minutes, getting adjusted to the music, but opened them when I felt someone's hip sliding against my thigh. I looked, to find Frankie smiling at me. "You look really hot tonight. I don't know what's wrong with these women."

She danced away from me teasingly. I reached out and gently ran a finger down her back. Frankie turned and asked, "Do you know what you're doing?"

"Who, me? I'm not doing anything." My hand brushed her thigh. She responded by slowly licking her lips. I felt a flush spread through my body, and looked away. I finally smiled to myself, made a half-second decision, and said, "Let's give them something to look at. They look too bored."

Frankie winked at me. "All right, they won't forget us here."

I took her hand and we danced for a few minutes, just letting our bodies pick up the same rhythm. As she moved away from me, my hand slid across her breasts. She turned, grabbed my hips, and pushed her body into mine. I reached my hand out and tilted her chin up toward my face as she straddled my thigh, looking like we were going to have sex on the dance floor. I was dancing with my eyes closed again, oblivious of everything but the music and the heat from her body inches away.

The music changed and we kept dancing, smiling at each other as the crowd started to watch. The sweat was pouring off me. I felt my clothes clinging, and enjoyed every moment of being watched with lust by the same women who had ignored us an hour ago. Frankie was enjoying it, too. The record changed again, and she growled like a feline in heat. I threw my head back and laughed as we left the dance floor and walked straight out the door, never looking back.

Once outside, we jumped into a waiting cab and started laughing so hard I couldn't tell the driver where to go. We managed somehow to make it home. With a sigh of relief I let us into my apartment. As I closed the door, Frankie leaned me against the wall, slowly kissing me on the mouth. The blood started rushing through my veins again. I turned away, embarrassed by the flush of emotion I felt. We were just friends. I never expected or even considered anything else. True, we were good friends, but after the death of her lover and my best friend, Royce, I'd always thought of myself as her protector. I told her I couldn't deal with any more that night. I wanted to get some sleep and we'd talk in the morning. This was all so unexpected, I was afraid I'd do something out of rashness that would change our friendship too much.

I pulled my clothes off and reached in the closet for a clean T-shirt, keeping my back to her as I pulled it over my head.

This is silly, I thought. We've seen each other undressed many times. I shouldn't be feeling this way. I went into the bathroom to wash up, then climbed the stepladder to the loft bed and found that Frankie had already gotten in, wrapped the sheet around her, and was staring up at the stars out the window over the bed.

I got in and lay as close to the edge as possible without falling off. We lay there silently until an airplane crossed over; we said good night and rolled over, our backs just inches apart.

I got up with the sun, not having slept well. Every time either of us moved we seemed to brush together, and every time we brushed together an electric shock ran through me. The shock woke me completely, at least a hundred times. Deciding the best thing to do was take a shower, I took my clothes and marched to the bathroom. The water felt wonderful. I stood and let the spray run down my back while I soaped and resoaped my breasts and stomach. I found myself daydreaming that someone else was seducing me with the bar of soap. Reluctantly, I changed the shower to cold water. After my hair dried and teeth were brushed, there was no reason to stay in the bathroom any longer. I decided to see if Frankie was awake.

The door to the loft bed was open, and I stood watching the scene on the bed. The sun was coming up golden through the curtain of plants in the window. Frankie was awake. She was kneeling, with her back to me. Her hands were absentmindedly playing with the spider plant. The sheet had dropped off and was lying in a pile on the bed; the sun and plants were silhouetting her nude body in the morning glow.

I crossed the room to the bed.

The DOZENS

bitch
hoe
yo mama
yo sistah…

Jessie and Virgie were down by the railroad tracks in back of the abandoned hat factory playing the dozens again. It was a game they had played since grade school and usually went on and on until you ran out of relatives or somebody got punched out for saying something bad about somebody's mama.

The game was going good until Jessie decided to add a little twist to the tellin'….

Jessie secretly wanted to love Virgie like a man loves a woman, but never had the courage to tell her, let alone touch her. Her nights were filled with longing for Virgie and now the "dozens" was her chance to make it happen.

She also knew that Virgie was hotheaded and if she made her mad enough she could challenge her to a dare.

Yeah, Jessie thought, *Virgie would never back down from a dare.*

yo mama sucks pussy
yo...

"Hey! What you mean my mama suck pussy? Bitch, I'ma fuck you up talkin' bout my mama like that."

"Yeah? You and who else?"

Virgie got right up in Jessie's face. She didn't feel good about fighting Jessie because Jessie was a big, tough tomboy and would probably stomp her to the ground, but on the other hand she didn't want to lose face, either.

Her Lola Delores from the Philippines had always told her to never lose face. That was the worst thing any Filipina could have happen to her.

"If my mama sucks pussy, then your mama sucks dick."

"Humph..." Jessie was getting mad now. "I'd rather my mama suck dick than some ole tired pussy."

"How you know if she like dick instead of pussy? Huh? You suck any dick or pussy lately?"

"No, but if you let me suck your pussy then maybe I'll know."

The game was getting hot and the odds were in Jessie's favor.

"So what's happening here? You gonna let me suck your pussy?"

"You really mean it, don't you, Jessie?"

Now Virgie was getting nervous because she also had the desire for Jessie and often fantasized it was Jessie's finger touching her under the covers at night.

"I'll come by tonight after your mom goes to work and I dare you."

That night Jessie opened her mouth to her first taste of sin and Virgie moaned under her. The taste was bittersweet on her tongue and she liked it when Virgie's juice filled her mouth, and she swallowed hard to keep up with Virgie's back-and-forth motion.

"Oh, girl, you're so good at this. I'm gonna let you suck me every day."

"If you like it so much, why don't you sit on my face?"

Virgie obliged and came, crashing down on Jessie's face.

"Virg, you ever fuck?" Jessie was horny and eager to put her hand where her mouth was.

Virgie lay on her back, but Jessie turned her on her stomach and held her ass tight as she started to hand-fuck her.

Virgie came in a minute, but Jessie continued to fuck not only her cunt, but her ass at the same time. Virgie was sore but she experienced pleasure from all openings in her body.

Jessie turned her onto her back again and sucked hard on her nipples while she pumped her own cunt on Virgie's leg and continued to fuck her with her own pumping rhythm.

The next day they did not play the dozens and it was a long time before Virgie allowed herself to face Jessie again.

They made love a few more times before Virgie went off to college and Jessie went to jail.

Before Virgie left, she made Jessie promise.

"Promise me you won't tell anybody I let you suck my pussy."

"I did more than that—I fucked you, didn't I, and you liked it, too."

Four years went by and Virgie came home. Somehow Jessie found out and was waiting for her at the train station. She made a big show of affection and insisted on driving her to her door.

During the ride home Virgie learned that Jessie had been out of jail for about a year and was managing a small print shop and editing a newsletter for women in prison. Yes, she was still living with her mom and two younger sisters.

Damn, she looked *good.* Virgie promised to have a drink with her one night but, she added, please don't call me at my parents' house.

Jessie was known to have a lot of girls and was too much of a stud butch to hide her sexual orientation.

Now, since coming home, Virgie avoided her as much as possible.

Talk was cheap and, coming from a Catholic family, Virgie had too much to lose. They would never understand and so she stayed in the closet.

In college she had had a few flings with men, but none ignited the passion that Jessie had.

Just the mention of Jessie's name caused her heart to beat and made a warm wetness between her legs.

One afternoon she found herself down by the railroad tracks in back of the still-abandoned hat factory.

She found herself reminiscing that she was sixteen again and playing the dozens game with Jessie.

Virgie decided if she got through this day she would say five Hail Marys and make a novena to the Blessed Virgin Mother. But her knees shook just thinking about Jessie.

Hours later she found herself on Jessie's doorstep.

"Jessie!" She banged hard on the door. "Jessie, you in there?"

She was in a bad way and desperate enough not to care who saw her carrying on.

The door pushed open and there was Jessie rubbing the sleep out of her eyes.

"Damn, girl, what's the matter with you? Can't you see

everybody sleep around here; you gone crazy or some-thin'?"

Virgie thought, yes, crazy to let myself think I could forget you and crazy to let you go. She hoped it wasn't too late to rekindle the passion of four years gone by. She realized then that there might be someone waiting in Jessie's bed.

Virgie took a deep breath. "Jessie, do you have another girl?"

She looked deep into Jessie's eyes.

Jessie searched her soul but she knew in her heart that it belonged to Virgie.

She answered softly, "No."

Virgie pushed Jessie aside, walked into the house and straight to the couch that doubled as Jessie's sofabed.

Virgie was home to stay for as long as Jessie wanted her.

Smokey's STORY

Smokey looked for love in all the wrong places.

Once she showed up at the Hide-A-Way Bar on one of those nights. Looking for love. She found love all right....

Standing at the bar with a cigarette hanging out the side of her mouth and wearing a gray sharkskin suit stood Key; with those deep brown soulful eyes and full lips made for kissing girls in all the right places. Key was known for picking up girls like Smokey. With a practiced eye Key looked Smokey up and down, with a look that promised everything.

Smokey was excited by this butch who bought her a drink, talked low, whispered things in her ear, held her tight, led her to the dance floor, and ground her crotch in time to the music.

Then the finale as Key led Smokey out the door to the rhythm of "how'd you like to come home with me tonight?"

There was a look of danger in Key's eyes that made Smokey's body quiver with anticipation. Key took her hand without waiting for her answer, and seemed to take for granted that Smokey would follow her anywhere.

Key's car was like Key. Sleek, black, and with tinted windows made for seeing out, not in. As Smokey got into the front seat, Key leaned over and snapped the seat belt tight across Smokey's waist and breasts. Without speaking, she put the key into the ignition and turned up the stereo, and the car took off into the darkness of the city. Smokey thought they would spend the rest of the evening at Key's place, but as Key turned onto a deserted road outside the city limits she knew she might get more than she bargained for. Smokey suddenly realized she was in a car with a total stranger and no way out unless Key opened the door. It was one of those converted police cars with no door handles and could only be opened with a key—and the driver held it. Smokey struggled to get out of the seat belt, but found herself in restraints.

The car had stopped in the middle of nowhere. No houses, no lights, no people. Key reached over and ran her hand up and down Smokey's breasts. With her other hand she parted her legs, pulled her pantyhose down along with her panties, and slipped a probing finger into Smokey's cunt. Key still hadn't said a word since they left the bar.

All Smokey could hear was her heavy breathing as she ripped her dress down and across, baring her breast to Key's mouth. Smokey felt powerless to say no as Key sucked hard on her nipple and plunged one, then four fingers into Smokey's dripping pussy. Finally her entire hand entered and she fucked her hard. Smokey struggled to keep her legs together, but she had never been fucked like this before. It was exciting being made love to in the front seat of a car with a total stranger. All at once she felt her juices running down the crack of her ass onto the leather seat cover. With her other hand Key felt for the mechanism that dropped the seat practically to the floor. Smokey felt her head touching the backseat as Key withdrew her hand from her throbbing pussy. She was getting close to coming, and begged Key not to stop. Key slapped her once across the face, then pulled her dress up around her waist, exposing her naked cunt.

Smokey cried out, but Key covered her mouth with kisses and parted her legs once more. Smokey was scared. This was all getting out of hand, but Key had total control as she laid her body on top of Smokey's and forced her hand to the hardness of her crotch. Smokey felt violated when Key pulled her zipper down, took out her hard cock, and entered her. The kissing stopped abruptly as Key put her hand over Smokey's mouth. Key pumped long, hard strokes into Smokey's center. Smokey willed her to stop, as it would be impossible to stop her physically. After a while she lost all sense of time, and the fucking seemed endless. Her mind screamed rape, but was it? She had never been raped by a woman before, but had never experienced anyone as aggressive as Key. Smokey tried to make sense of the whole situation, but there was an urgent need between her legs and she knew she had to come before Key was spent. She tried to imagine how Key's cock would feel in her ass.

Somewhere between night and day Smokey passed out.

She remembered Key undoing the straps, pulling her panties up, and pinning her dress over her exposed breasts. She thought she dreamed that Key picked her up, carried her to her car, laid her gently on the backseat, put a coat over her, kissed her. Yes, she must be dreaming. Dreaming of a woman who put her cock in her mouth, and fucked her so hard it drove her to the edge of madness. Dreaming strange erotic dreams of sex with a stranger. "Key," she said out loud. Key.

45-MINUTE *Blowjob*

I had a hot date with this bitch one night—sucked my dick but made me wait forty-five minutes before she'd let me come.

She drove and I was in the passenger seat. Couldn't wait to get her home so I could fuck her in my own driver's seat. But the broad had other plans....

We stopped at every red light along the avenue while she went down on my dick. Finally she parked at a secluded spot just under the Golden Gate Bridge. Just as the action was getting hot and steamy a cop car flashed its lights and pulled up beside us.

"C'mon, baby," she says, "put your dick back in your pants."

Well, by that time I had such a hard-on my nine-inch cock wouldn't go back in my jockey shorts and I couldn't pull my zipper up. I sat there holding my cock as best as I could, trying to stroke it on the sly. Then the bitch tells me, "If you make yourself come you can forget about fucking me or having your dick sucked later."

We drove on, stopping at several traffic lights, and headed for the beach.

Well, her tongue tantalized my shaft up and down, teased the head while her hand did slow strokes. I grabbed her hair to hold her mouth in place when her lips stopped their sucking motion. I was one minute short of coming when she looks at her watch and tells me, "Baby, you have ten minutes left before you can come. I'm sure you can hold out."

Being the butch that I am, I obliged, and ten minutes later came like my life depended on it. She rewarded me by working her mouth into a frenzy and making me come five more times. This was butch heaven in the front seat of a car, when she turned on the ignition and asked me, "Your place or mine?"

Of course I said "mine." I'd anticipated getting even by fucking her nonstop like an all-night 747 turbo jet.

My date was one step ahead of me by the time we got to my place.

She pulled her skirt up around her waist, slid her panties down, laid a big kiss on me, and said, "My number's listed in the phone book if you wanna call me." And drove off after shoving her wet lacy panties in my hand.

LORETTA

The first time I met Loretta I hated her. I was in the ninth grade at Franklin High School and hangin' out with the baddest girl gang in Philadelphia, the Ma Dragons.

One day we was all sittin' at the lunch table at school when this really tall white girl with bleached-blonde hair and a tryin'-to-be-cool attitude walked up and put her lunch tray on our table. None of us said anything, but we looked at her like we usually looked at any white chick tryin' to check us out. This usually kept a distance between us and them, but Loretta wasn't into backin' down.

There we were, the Ma Dragons—two blacks, two Puerto Ricans, an Italian–Puerto Rican, and me, a half-white Filipino who looked Puerto Rican—all starin' stone-faced at this crazy think-she-be-bad white bitch.

Loretta said, "If nobody's sitting here, then I am." And she sat down.

Now somebody had to do something. Nobody ever sat at our table without us tellin' them they could.

To make a long story short, me and Loretta agreed to

meet in the back of the Texaco gas station at eight o'clock that night.

While me and my girls was gettin' ready for the big fight, Loretta already knew she would kick my ass. My best friend, Tee-Tee Cooper, said she would jump in if things got too bad, but when she saw Loretta she cussed me out.

"Girl, you know who that is? That bitch you gon' be fightin' with is the leader of the Emeralds. I know that chick from reform school and she is one bad girlfriend. Loretta Vitale gon' whop your behind tonight!"

The fight lasted for about an hour and Loretta's friends kept askin' me if I was ready to stop the fight, and my friends kept tellin' me they'd jump in if I wanted them to. Well, I was a tough butch in those days, so I fought till I couldn't stand up. Till my eyes filled with blood and I couldn't see where I was swingin'. My friends got cold rags from the bathroom to wipe the blood from my face and Loretta's friends told me it was a good fight and congratulated me for "hanging tuff."

When I got home the first thing I did was look in a mirror.

My friends all told me I looked OK, but my face felt all different. I wondered if I would ever look the same again. Both eyes were black and blue, and one was swollen shut. My bottom lip was split, and when I ran my tongue behind my two front teeth they popped out. My nose was all swollen and still bleedin', but I didn't know it was broken till my pops took me to the hospital emergency room. Pops was really mad. When he found out I lost the fight he cussed me out in Visayan and slapped me once across the face. Then he made me sit in the kitchen and hold a piece of raw meat on my eyes while he called a taxi to take us to the hospital and cussed me some more. I didn't care too much, 'cause even though I lost the fight I didn't punk out, and now I had an even badder reputation. But in my head I swore I would never lose another fight again.

I didn't want to go to school the next day, but my pops made me. He was still yellin'.

"See how you look now, big shot. You want be big shot at school, well, you can stay in this house till I tell you to go out! No more hanging with your girlfriends every night!"

By the time I got to school everybody knew what happened, but it was like I was a hero or somethin'. Loretta and her girls caught up with me in the bathroom, and I pulled out my blade expectin' a fight, but all she wanted to do was shake hands and ask me if I wanted to join the Emeralds. Loretta's gang was all white—Irish and Italian. Even though I was half Irish, I didn't feel it. I told her no, and she said no hard feelings.

I grew up real fast that summer. Me and Loretta became friends, I flunked out of ninth grade, robbed a gas station, and did some time in reform school.

The last time I saw Loretta was in 1976. She was goin' to jail for manslaughter 'cause she killed this dude who used to be her boyfriend. He beat her up too many times so she shot him. Loretta never did like nobody messin' with her.

By that time I had been through a lot of changes. I had lost close friends through drugs, gang fights, and prison walls.

The Ma Dragons, however, would always be a part of my life from adolescence and into my adulthood. Some bonds can never be broken.

Jessie's SONG

I met Jessie in 1967 at The State Reformatory for Girls. She was the baddest girl I ever met and looked much older than her sixteen years. Her arms were scarred from her wrists to the elbow from knife fights and where she cut herself with razors. I heard she even took a straightedge to her own mother 'cause she wouldn't let Jessie have her way. Both her front teeth were knocked out from a fight she had with two male guards from another reform school, and she wore her hair man-style in a short 'fro, square in the back and close on the sides. Her eyes were what scared me. One eye went in one direction, while the other looked straight ahead. It was like she could see you at all times.

Anyway, I met Jessie while "standing on line." It was only my third day at the place and I got in trouble for talking back to a guard and refusing to go to church services. The punishment was to stand facing the wall, every day, for a week.

From 5:30 in the morning until 8:30 at night you ate, went to school, and worked standing. Jessie and I would look sideways at each other and talk about how we got locked up. Jessie told me she was in there for assault and battery on her ninth-grade teacher, petty theft, and truancy. I told her I was in for vandalizing a school, truancy, and robbing a gas station. She thought it was really cool that I had a gun when me and my two friends robbed the place. That was when we decided to be friends, and that was when the plan started. With the exception of one girl, nobody ever broke out of there, and that girl was only a legend 'cause nobody even knew her name.

When we got off line I found out Jessie and I were going to be dorm mates. The dormitory was divided into two groups: Group A for the older girls, and Group B for girls under fifteen. The groups were separated by an enclosed partition where the night guards watched us through four inches of glass. Cubicles lined both sides of the long room with two steel cots per cubicle and a thick mesh screen separating the two cots. Jessie and I whispered through the steel mesh and passed notes back and forth, eating them afterward. We watched the pattern of the guards coming and going for three months, timed how long it took the electronic doors to open and close, and related all sense of timing to music. Jessie thought of a way to talk in song, and each song meant something only to us. Me and Jessie had it all worked out. When it came time to break out of there we were gonna sing "Breaking Down the Walls of Heartache" and then run like hell.

We decided to take off one night after dinner. By this time it would be dark and they'd have a hard time finding us. It was winter, and the days were getting shorter. The setup was like this: after dinner we'd have a short recreation period outside, then they'd march us from the yard, through the back door of the kitchen, into the dining room, and we'd stand at attention while two housemothers called roll. By this time the back door of the kitchen would be locked and they'd begin dividing us into small groups of eight girls standing two by two. This group of eight would go through a metal door that automatically opened and closed. From there you stood in a small hallway until another electronic door opened that led to the staircase into the second-floor dormitory. The doors were set on a timer. When one opened, another one closed and locked behind you in just a matter of seconds. The only other door was an emergency exit in the dining room. This led directly outside into a side yard, and this was the door Jessie and I would go through.

We were the last two in line. Jessie and I were always a little late because I had kitchen duty while Jessie cleaned the yard and washed garbage cans. We were gonna run in between the time it took for the first door to close behind us and the second one to open.

We just stepped into the hallway when Jessie started to sing the first couple of words from "Breaking Down the Walls of Heartache." There was eight seconds left to get through the door before it locked us in.

"Oh, God," I prayed. "Don't let me slip in the snow."

I heard the dogs barking behind us and we struggled to run faster. There were rumors that the fence was electrified. Sweat dripped from Jessie's face and there was a look of terror in her eyes like that of a condemned killer going to the electric chair. I never saw Jessie scared of anything until now. She was like a stranger beside me. Neither of us spoke, but I could hear our breath lingering in the air and hearts pounding so fast I was afraid they'd burst from fear and exertion. Jessie and I wanted our freedom so badly that it overcame our fear, and we made it to the fence.

The fence turned out to be two cyclone fences spaced fifteen feet apart, twelve feet tall, and topped with six inches of barbed wire. I remembered seeing a movie once about a jailbreak, and this guy threw a wet coin against the fence to test the electricity. I thought about scooping up a handful of snow and throwing it like he did in the movie, but we were desperate now and somehow the thought of death didn't bother me as much as being in that place did. I just wanted out. I wanted to hang with my friends and see my girl again. So I gritted my teeth and tried to look tough for all the other girls we left behind. If we were gonna die it would be cool. I jumped and grabbed cold metal. For one second I felt faint 'cause I thought the icy steel was the feeling of electricity on my hand. I looked for Jessie and she was there beside me. She gave me a nod and we continued our climb. First to the top, then hold on, then swing your legs over the barb wire. Climb down the other side halfway and then jump. We had rehearsed this whole thing in our minds every day for the past three months, but I never really thought we'd be doing this. We made it over the first fence easily. By the time we got to the second one I thought my lungs would give out. Jessie's size and bulk made it harder for her, and she caught herself on the jagged wire. I made it over the top with just one tear in my pants, but I noticed blood coming from Jessie's arm. I started the rehearsal in my mind again. Just a few more steps and jump... We hit the ground! I ran harder. No time to help Jessie now. I only hoped she didn't leave a trail of blood for the dogs to follow, but if we turned to look it would only slow us down. I knew there was a gas station and a 7-Eleven store just across the highway. An old friend of mine from school hung out there. If we could only get across we were home free. If...if we ever made it that far.

I forced my feet to move faster. They were frozen with pain. I didn't have socks on and the wet snow had seeped through my canvas sneakers. I was shaking. The only other things I had on were a white T-shirt with the number A-17 stenciled on the front and a pair of dungaree work pants.

We made it to the gas station, and I was right. There was a buch of kids, boys and girls around our age, in the back smoking dope and drinking beer. A couple of the girls were wearing Emerald colors. Jessie and I didn't have to explain ourselves. Everybody from around there knew about the reform school, and me and Jessie looked like we were on the run. One of the Emerald chicks was checking us out. She kinda looked familiar, like one of the seniors at my old high school. She looked at me like maybe she knew me, too.

"Hey, you from the reform school?"

"Yeah. You gotta help us. I'm friends with one of your girls. You know Loretta?" Jessie and I were in a hurry so I didn't waste too much time with words.

"Yeah, we know her, so what?"

Now I was getting impatient, and I could see that Jessie was in a worse mood than I was.

"Look, all we need is a ride to the bus and some carfare. Can you help us or what?"

This other girl looked at me real hard and asked where I knew Loretta from.

They weren't comfortable with us yet, and I knew Jessie was gonna start swinging soon if we didn't get out of there. I thought fast.

"I had a fight with Loretta last year in back of the gas station. Me and her's cool now."

The girl who looked familiar checked me out again. "Your name Stoney? 'Cause if it is then you're OK with me." She turned around and looked at her girls. "Stoney hangs with the Ma Dragons and she's tight with Loretta."

One of the guys told us to get in his car. He was gonna drive us to a bus stop out of the neighborhood. The girl who said she knew me gave us a pack of cigarettes and a couple of dollars, and this big guy gave me his hooded sweatshirt. Jessie's new outfit fit her and she was able to wear an old pair of boots that somebody stole from the mechanic. My outfit was three times bigger than me, but with the hood up I passed for a little boy. We promised to give the clothes back someday, but I knew we'd never see those white kids again. Some of them looked at us like they'd never seen a black person or a Filipino before.

Jessie wanted to hide out at her grandma's place and all I could think about was seein' my girlfriend Carmen.

"All you think about is your other friend. Fuck this girl, we goin' to my house 'cause you ain't gettin' off this bus without me." Jessie pulled a knife out of her pocket that she had taken from the boy's car and held it against my back. I knew she would stab me in a minute if she didn't get her way. I had seen her in enough fights and knew she meant every word. Jessie was the kind of girl that would kill her own mother if she fucked with her. I lit a cigarette and we didn't talk the rest of the way.

Jessie's grandma lived in the last house on a dead-end street. It was a row home with a sagging porch, and brown paint peeling from the wooden shingles. The door was open and we went in.

"Who there?" Jessie's grandma yelled from the bedroom that was next to the kitchen. The door was open partway and I could just make out a small dark figure illuminated from the TV set, sitting on the edge of the bed. Jessie told me to wait in the kitchen while she talked to her grandma.

I sat down and lit a cigarette and looked over my new surroundings, trying to figure out a way to get out of there.

The stovetop and the walls around it were covered with layers of old grease, but the floor was clean, although patches of linoleum had come up, and was covered with tar paper and black electrical tape. Everything looked like it had seen better days except for the dandelions in old Thunderbird wine bottles. The window over the sink faced a small yard littered with green plastic trash bags, broken glass, and beer bottles, and enclosed with a rusted chain-link fence.

I realized I missed my father's house with his clean kitchen, the smell of fish and *pancit,* and the scent of roses in the backyard. I tried to make a phone call but the line was dead. Jessie told me later that the service had been cut off months ago, and I felt more like a prisoner here than in reform school.

All of a sudden I heard Jessie and her grandma arguing over something. I could hear Jessie telling her we were only going to stay for a few days, and her grandma telling her she didn't want any trouble.

"I don' want no kinda trouble 'round here! You hear me, Jess? You can stay, but I want your light-skinned friend outta my house. Ain't havin' no kinda trouble from the police. You think you bad, don't you, Jess? Just come bargin' on in here with one of your little gal friends. You think I don't know what's goin' on? Just 'cause I'm a old lady don't mean that I ain't slick. You damn near killed your mama and one a these days you gon' be the death of me."

The door flew open and Jessie's grandma came into the kitchen. I jumped up from where I was sitting and put my cigarette out. She pointed her finger at me.

"Look, you can stay till the mornin' and then I want you outta my house. I don't know what you is, but I know you ain't got no business messin' round here."

She turned to look at Jessie standing behind her. "You can sleep in the other bedroom with Crystal, but your friend here got to stay on the couch. And she gotta be out by the time I gets back from church. You hear me, Jessie? And I ain't got nothin' to eat but some fatback and white bread."

Jessie's grandma went back to her bedroom, still mumbling. "Filipino humph, she look Puerto Rican if you ask me. Whoever thought of a Filipino in a black neighborhood? Well, I ain't gonna be the first one to have them in my house!" And she slammed the door.

Jessie sat down and put her head on the table; it was a long time before we spoke again. I felt I lost my only friend.

It wasn't until Jessie's nineteen-year-old cousin, Crystal, came by that I felt some kind of excitement. I immediately forgot all about my troubles, because for now Crystal was my ticket out of that hell.

Crystal stood up to her full height, all five feet four inches of her. She was all woman, and for a minute I thought I was staring at my fantasy woman, Tina Turner. Crystal put both hands on her hips and looked me dead in the eye.

"I want you to eat my pussy."

Jessie was getting mad. "Hey Crystal, she don' wanna be bothered with you. Stop makin' up shit and get yo' black ass in that bedroom."

"Shit. She look like a baby butch to me, and I like 'em young. So tell me, Stoney, do you eat pussy or what?"

I didn't know what to say, so I didn't say anything. I wasn't even sure that Jessie was a dyke, and she didn't know too much about me, either. How could I tell her I ached to fuck her cousin? Jessie would kill me.

Crystal looked me up and down, around and across, but I didn't mind. She was the finest chick I'd ever seen.

"Yeah, I'm lookin' at you. That your name, ain't it, Stoney?" She said it like an accusation. "And I ain't wastin' no time talkin' no jive. You eat pussy or what?"

Jessie took Crystal by the arm, shoving her into the

bedroom. As the door closed I could hear Crystal laughing. I sighed, got under the blankets on the couch, and tried to sleep. I laid awake for a while thinking about fucking Crystal, but I was so tired and my body was too sore to stay up any longer.

I fell asleep in the middle of my fantasy.

I don't know how long I slept; it was still dark when I woke to find Crystal slipping under the covers with me. I groaned inwardly when I felt she had nothing on under a thin cotton bathrobe. I wanted to feel her large breasts in my hands and mouth. She must have read my mind as she opened her robe and let her breasts touch my face. I started to suck, gently at first, but my mouth was hungry and demanded more. And then Crystal started to moan as I sucked harder, trying to pull her whole breast into my mouth.

"C'mon, baby, let's go on in the bedroom. If you keep suckin' my titties like that I'm gonna wake the whole neighborhood."

"But what about Jessie?"

"Fuck Jessie. She sleepin', ain't she? If Jessie wanna fuck she'll wake up."

It was just what I was afraid of. Jessie waking up. I wanted Crystal really bad, but not enough to fuck Jessie, too. Crystal made the decision by putting my hand up her robe, between her legs, and into her dark wetness.

Jessie was snoring as Crystal pulled me on top of her. By this time she was completely naked and my sixteen-year-old mind wished I had a cock so I could ride her to heaven.

"So, Stoney, you ready to eat my pussy?"

I answered by putting my head between her legs. Crystal's clit was large, and I sucked it between my lips until she couldn't stand it anymore.

"Girl, you gonna make me come doin' me like that!"

I stopped sucking, but my tongue slowly stroked her hard clit up and down. Crystal put a pillow over her face and I was so busy licking that I didn't notice Jessie was up and watching until Crystal came, and I felt someone pulling my head from between her legs. Wham! Jessie back-handed the side of my head.

"Bitch! I tell you you could eat my cous'?"

Crystal held on to Jessie and tried to calm her.

"Shh. C'mon, baby, slow down. Mama's gon' wake up and throw us all out the house if she hear all this commotion."

Jessie put her hands around my throat and started squeezing.

Crystal was pleading. "OK, OK, baby. I did you wrong, but I thought you'd get some from Stoney, too. Right, Stoney? Ain't you gonna give Jessie a little pussy?"

I was *not* gonna give it up to Jessie. She was going to have to kill me in her grandma's house, and in her grandma's bed first. Jessie must have been reading my mind because she squeezed harder and I started choking.

"You done lost yo' mind, girl! You gon' kill this chile' right in the bed. I'ma have to scream, Jess, and then the police gon' take you right out and straight to the 'lectric chair!"

Slap! Jessie sent Crystal sailing off the bed and clear across the room. She looked at me with that cross-eyed glare.

"Bitch, take yo' muthfuckin' clothes off and fuck that bitch. I wanna watch."

Crystal smiled wickedly and came over to the bed like they had been all through this before. She took a leather strap and a dildo out of the nightstand and threw them on the bed.

"Let's see how bad you are with this."

It was my worst nightmare. I didn't know if I was supposed

to do Crystal, or if Crystal was gonna do me. I didn't even know how to use one of those things. I always wanted one to try it on Carmen, but you had to be twenty-one to get into the porno place where they sold them.

This was really embarrassing. I wished I could go into the bathroom and put it on under my clothes, but I'd have to play this off big-time because Jessie wasn't letting me out of her sight.

Crystal must have known because she started tugging on my pants. "C'mon, baby, let me help you. Ol' Crystal gonna get you strapped on and then give you the best ride of your life. I'm gonna enjoy every minute of it if you can fuck as good as you eat pussy."

I got enough of my confidence back to tell her I didn't need any help, and I knew how to please a woman.

This made Jessie mad all over again, and she started after me. "Bitch, I tell you you could talk to my woman like that?"

Crystal got between us, trying to pull Jessie off of me. "You lay one hand on her, Jessie, and I'll kill you. I'm the one who pays the rent around here and sends you money every week. And I ain't yo' woman, Jess, I'm everybody's woman when it gets right down to it. Do I have to remind you where that money comes from? Answer me, Jess. Do I?"

Jessie got quiet after that and went out of the room.

I wanted to ask Crystal what she meant, but she put her arms around me and led me to the bed.

"Now, Stoney, you gonna show me how you please a woman?"

My first experience fucking like that was everything and more than what I expected. Jessie came in after we had been fucking for five hours and just as coolly lit a cigarette and sat on the bed staring at the TV set while we went at it hot and heavy.

Crystal had explained to me that it was "their thing." Her and Jessie used to trick together before Jessie went to reform school. These guys would come over there and pay money just to watch them fuck. Now Crystal turned tricks by herself while grandma went to church and looked the other way, and Crystal paid the rent by fucking.

I was sad to hear that, 'cause Crystal was such a pretty girl and so young.

"Hey, Crystal, you ever been in love?"

"Oh, yeah, baby. Every time I pull my panties down and gets that green laid in my palm, I'm in love—straight to the bank!"

We fucked our brains out till the sun came up.

I had just enough time to lay back down on the couch when Jessie's grandma got up. I could hear her banging around in the kitchen looking for matches to light the stove, because other than that, there wasn't any heat in the house. I shivered, pulled the covers over my head, and wished I could get back in the bed with Crystal. With, or without Jessie, I wanted to be with her again. Was I falling in love with her? And Carmen, what was I gonna do about Carmen? We'd been going steady since fifth grade until I got locked up, and now I heard she was seeing this white guy. It wasn't my fault we couldn't be together all these months. I thought she would wait for me. Now that I'm out of there I'm stuck with this crazy Jessie.

I wanted to go to sleep, but Jessie's grandma started yelling. "Come on, Jess, wake up! I know you got matches in there. And Crystal you better get on down to the oil company and pay this bill before we all freeze to death. Jessie, you hear me? I know you 'wake in there. And this house better be cleaned up and your friend off a my couch before I get back. Ain't havin' no watcha-ma-call-its in my house!"

I must have dozed off because the next thing I knew Jessie was hitting me, and Crystal had gone out for coffee.

"Get up, Stoney. You can't sleep here all day! We gonna get put out if you still here when mama get back."

I sat up as Crystal came in the door carrying two bags of groceries. She tossed me a pack of cigarettes. "Here, Stoney, I hope y'all smoke Kools, 'cause that's the last pack I'ma buy for you, and I got y'all some coffee."

"Crystal! Yo, Crystal! Make me some food, girl! And gimme some cigarettes, too."

Crystal must have been in a really bad mood because after she put the groceries away she came out of the kitchen with a paring knife in her hand and headed straight for Jessie. She waved the knife in Jessie's face and cussed her out. "Look, Jess, I don't see your ugly ass fuckin' nobody. If you wanna eat, cook it yourself, bitch. I'm sick of you and mama tellin' me what to do. And another thing—your friend got to pay me for last night!" Crystal winked at me. "Maybe I'll just take it out in trade just 'cause I like you. I ain't never fucked with no Puerto Rican before!"

Now it was my turn to be mad. "I ain't *no* Puerto Rican."

Crystal laughed and strutted herself back to the kitchen, her hips swaying from side to side. "Look, I don't care what you is, but you sure is good!"

We finished eating, but I didn't feel any better about being there. I wished Jessie would give me some bus fare to get home. I wanted to sleep in my own bed with my own girlfriend and not have to worry about Jessie watching us or having to pay somebody for sex. My dad would be really upset that I ran away, but deep down he would be glad to see me and I knew he would never turn me in to the police. By now I'm sure every cop in the city was looking for us, and it was kind of exciting thinking about it. I wondered if Carmen knew I was out on the street.

If I had any thoughts about getting away, Jessie didn't want to hear about it. She looked at Crystal. "So what we gonna do 'bout Stoney?"

"Why Stoney gotta be here anyway? Don't she have a home?"

"I told you..." Jessie banged her fist on the table. "I'ma kill Stoney if she leave me."

That was it. I was going to have to fight Jessie in her grandma's kitchen. I stood up. "Look, I'm gettin' out of here right now and you can't stop me, Jess! Your grandma don't want me here, anyway!" I walked to the front door, Jessie right behind me. "If you want to fight me, Jess, go right ahead. I thought we were friends." I went into a fighting stance, my legs apart and hands balled into a fist. I ducked the first punch from Jessie, and then we went at it for real, fists pounding each other. We were used to this kind of fighting because girls fought like this every day at reform school. It was no big thing; we'd fight, get it over with, and be friends again. Jessie and I were wrestling on the floor when Crystal grabbed me by my shirt and pulled me away. "Tha's enough fightin'! You two gon' kill each other! Mama gon' be home soon and I ain't gettin' my black ass put outta here 'cause you two are tearin' up the place. Now, y'all better act right and help me get this place cleaned up before she get here."

After we washed the dishes and mopped the kitchen floor we went into Crystal's room. The bed was made, but Crystal was naked and examining herself in the mirror. Jessie came up behind her and ran her hands up and down the length of Crystal's body. She slapped Jessie's hands away. "Stop, Jess! I gotta get ready to go out. Stoney, you put a big ole hickey on my neck and now I'ma have to cover it up with makeup."

Jessie was persistent and continued playing with Crystal's nipples. I was getting jealous watching her. Jessie kissed her on the back of the neck and held her tight. "C'mon, baby, gimme some pussy. It ain't gonna take more than a minute."

"That's right, Jessie! It ain't gonna take more than a minute 'cause you ain't gettin' none!"

"Where you think you goin', anyway?"

Crystal covered herself with a robe and laid some clothes out on the bed. "Out, to make some money, Jess. I'm tired of bein' cold, and somebody gotta pay this oil bill. So if you want some pussy you better go on down to Denise's house and get you some!"

Jessie took what little money Crystal had and we walked two blocks around the corner to Denise's house. Jessie told me that Denise was her thirty-year-old lover and she would let us stay there. But Denise was not at all happy to see Jessie. She had just gotten out of bed and out of the arms of her latest lover, when Jessie pounded on the door. Her new lover had just enough time to wipe the cum off her face when Jessie put her fist through the window, reached in, and unlocked the door.

There was a big scene in the living room between Denise and Jessie. Jessie took one look at Denise, who was dressed only in a bra and jeans, and then went bounding up the stairs to the bedroom and found Denise's new butch still lying in bed wearing only a pair of jockey briefs. Jessie was on her in a minute, and the two of them tumbled off the bed. Denise was right behind her and had taken a gun out from her butch's pants.

"Jess, don't make me have to shoot you! This is my house and if I want somebody in my bed it's my choice. Now get the fuck out!"

Jessie took one last punch at Denise's lover, and got up off the floor.

"Pussy muthafucker. I'll get your ass outside when your girlfriend ain't around."

The big butch went to reach for Jessie, and Denise threatened to blow everybody away.

"Du-Wayne! If you can't act right you can get out with Jessie. I don't need either one of y'all destroying my things. I'm a grown woman and this is my house, and if you can't respect me then y'all can go to hell! Du-Wayne, don't get me wrong. I ain't makin' no excuses for Jessie, but she been away for a while and didn't know you and me been seein' each other." Denise smiled and bent over so Du-Wayne could see all of her cleavage. "Just get back in the bed, baby, and when I come back I'll make it all up to you."

I wished Denise would just shoot Jessie so I could get out of there. All this drama was making me think about Carmen, and the jealousy was killing me inside. For months I tried to get a letter to her, but our mail was censored and I couldn't say what I wanted to say. It wasn't till my cousin came to see me that I found out Carmen was going with this guy from our neighborhood. Where was Carmen now that I needed her? I was sixteen years old, with no place to go, no job, and my girlfriend was probably gettin' it on right now with this corner boy. God, I could still smell her. I thought about her every night when I hugged my pillow, pretending it was Carmen. I wanted to cry right now, but I'd have to save it for some other time when nobody could see me. Maybe I could steal Du-Wayne's gun and go down to Carmen's and shoot her man in front of all his corner boys. See how Carmen would like that. And then I'd kill myself right in front of her. See how she'd like to have nobody. Just like me. I had nobody now.

Jessie was still cussin' all the way downstairs. Denise took her arm and pulled her into the kitchen. "Jessie, what are you doing here and who's your friend? I thought them muthafuckers locked you up and threw away the key this time! Look, Jess, if you took off from that place I can't keep you here. Me and Du-Wayne is plannin' to get our own place. Du-Wayne got a good job and I ain't givin' her up."

Jessie was still trying to get Denise to change her mind. She pleaded, "C'mon, baby, give me another chance. I'll be so good to you Du-Wayne gonna look like a chump next to me."

Denise laughed. "Jess, you still talkin' big time. You ain't nothin' but a sixteen-year-old kid with nothin' happenin' but a police record and a pimp's rap! Go back to Crystal and your grandma, baby."

Jessie wasn't budging, but Denise still held the gun and told her in so many words to get out. We left after that and Jessie threw a rock into Denise's living-room window.

"OK, bitch! I'll get outta your life! But when Du-Wayne leave you for some other ho', don't come cryin' back to me. 'Cause Jessie ain't never gonna take you back. Your pussy ain't nothin' to me. You hear me, bitch? I can get all the pussy I want from all kinds of girls!"

We finally made it into an abandoned building a few doors from Denise's house. Jessie said we could hide out there till we got enough money together to leave town. In the meantime we could clean it up and get some blankets and stuff from her grandma's.

Three days later we were still living in the place. Jessie had set up her bedroom in the basement and mine was on the second floor. We stuck candles in old wine bottles, swept and mopped the floors, and cleaned as much as we could. A couple of junkies had been living there before us and we tossed out old torn-up mattresses that were covered with piss and cum stains. We threw out all the syringes and broken glass. It was really depressing, but it was home now. Crystal came by every day to drop off money and clothes. I had fixed my room up as nice as possible and made a bed out of boards, bricks, newspaper, and blankets. The last time I saw Crystal, we made love and she told me I was sweet, and I should stay that way. I wished Crystal wasn't a prostitute and I wished I was older so I could take care of her.

One day I had enough of it. I wasn't going to live in a vacant building with Jessie and hide out during the day, and wander the streets at night dodging police cars. I was tired of being hungry and dirty most of the time. Jessie kept promising we were gonna take a bus down to Atlantic City, but we never had enough money.

Once, when Jessie went to the store for food, I started throwing bottles out the second-floor window. I was hoping the people who lived across the street would call the police and I could turn myself in. I did this a couple of times and one afternoon when Jessie was sleeping I threw all the bottles with the candles out the window along with the bricks from my bed. Jessie was awake by the time the police cars pulled up, and had taken off out the back door and was climbing the fence that faced the alley. A policewoman from the Juvenile Aid Division caught her as two policemen were cuffing my hands behind my back. They knew right away who we were 'cause they had an APB on the wire with our descriptions. The cops were joking. "Hey, you're the two kids from the reform school. We been lookin' for you two for almost three weeks now. You girls hungry? We'll fix ya' up with a sandwich and then lock you up for the night. Ha. Ha. Let's see how you like staying in a real jail!"

Me and Jessie were given baloney sandwiches and then locked in this little cell that looked like a cage. There were two benches just wide enough to lie on, and the toilet was out in the open where everybody could see us. They had to cuff Jessie to one of the benches 'cause she wanted to fight with me for turning us in, but I was still scared she'd get loose and kill me during the night.

The next evening they took us back to the reform school after we saw this judge, and some prison doctor, to make sure we weren't pregnant or anything. Jessie and I didn't say a word on the ride back, and the last time I saw her was when they separated us and put us in solitary. I was really lonely and wished we could still be friends, but when my punishment was over I found out they had Jessie locked up in some mental ward over at the Byberry State Hospital.

I used to pass that way when I got older, when I had my own car. I tried to imagine what Jessie must look like, if she ever got out, if her and Denise ever got back together, and did she ever think about me?

It took me till I was twenty-three years old to ride past the place where Crystal lived, but the house was vacant and boarded up like all the other houses on that street.

GIRLFRIENDS

A story about love, suspense, and sex between women!

Preface

For those women (and you know who you are) that are not ex-lovers or friends of Pearly Does, the following characters may offend and shock you or make you laugh and cry and create a great deal of confusion throughout this story.

It is because of the above reasons that I have attempted to define the relationships/friendships between *Girlfriends* and eliminate some of the chaos....

Friends and Lovers:

Miz Pearly (The Heroine). Formerly lived in Philadelphia all of her life.

Was best friends with Wilnona Will until moving to New York City to pursue a writing career. She met Miss Nadine on the Lower East Side and they lived together for five years until Nadine started sleeping around (which is where the story begins—after their breakup).

Mae-Mae (also known as Mae Might). Wilnona Will's older sister. Also from Philadelphia, but quit school at age sixteen and ran away to New York City with a big bad butch named Bessie. They've been married now for twenty-eight years, but Mae-Mae is getting tired of Bessie's "thang." When Pearly and Nadine got together, Mae-Mae got them an apartment next to hers (so she could "keep an ear on things"). Mae-Mae *loves* to gossip.

Wilnona Will (younger sister of Mae Might and mother of Missy-Mae). Age forty-one, single, attractive, and celibate for the past two years. Miz Pearly's friend (and true love) in Philadelphia.

Nadine (the Villainess). Miz Pearly's ex-lover. Nuff said!

Missy-Mae (Wilnona's daughter).

Bessie (Mae-Mae's butch lover).

Ci-Ci Can (Villainess #2 and Wilnona's new lover).

Miss Frank (Prez of Les Femmes Unies, a social group for lesbians of color in Philadelphia). Friend of everyone (except Nadine).

Lucy (Wilnona's best friend).

Dear Wilnona,

  You just gotta talk to Miz Pearly. *Her and Miss Nadine broke up.*

  I'm so sick about it and Miz Pearly so sick that she shut herself up in her room and *never* comin' out again.

  I been slippin' food under her door but she ain't eat anything, won't take a bath, and I don't think she even slept for a coupla days. She just cry all the time and won't talk to nobody ('cept Nadine). And Miss Nadine, all she wanna do is go out dancin' and carryin' on. She act like nothin' botherin' her at all. It's so hard to believe.

  Please call and see if you can talk some sense to Pearly before she do somethin' that I don't even wanna think about.

                              Love, your worried sister,
                                          Mae-Mae

P.S.

  Maybe Missy-Mae can get her to laugh. She sure need a good one now!

February 14, 1986

My dear Wilnona,
    Well, it's been a month since Nadine and I broke up.
    I'm sorry I didn't write sooner, but I needed the time alone without distractions and most of all to clear my head of all the anguish.
    Life here is slow. I live by myself in the desert, writing and teaching poetry to Indian children. I'm still not sure what direction my life will take in the near future. I've written to Nadine every day asking her for a reconciliation, but my letters go unanswered. Mae-Mae called and told me Nadine has been seeing someone else, and they seem really happy.
    As for me, I plan to stay far away from relationships and all women for the rest of my life! The only woman I feel good around (since Nadine) is you. I really miss you a lot and think about you every day. I'll be writing to you again when I'm feeling better.

Love,
Pearl

April 8, 1986

Dear Wilnona,

    Lord have mercy! Miz Pearly comin' home! She be gettin' off the plane this comin' Friday at twelve o'clock in the afternoon. I guess she don't wanna miss the Les Femmes dance that Miss Frank givin' on the 27th. I just can't wait to see her! I been missin' Pearly somethin' fierce and it sure be good to have her back.

                    Love, your happy sister,
                          Mae-Might

P.S.
    Maybe you two can hook up now.

April 13, 1986

Dear Wilnona,

   Miz Pearly home now and girlfriend sure lookin' fine. Me and Bessie (I had to drag her along like a dog) went to get her from the airport. And that ole nasty Nadine didn't even miss her all this time and been lookin' sad now that Pearly back in town. Well, they's livin' together again, but it don't look like they ever gonna be lovers again. Miss Nadine still runnin' around. She got two gals and one boyfriend. And Miz Pearly say she gonna run around, too (cept she only go out with gals). I'm thinkin' she gonna visit with you soon. Ha! You still ain't doin' it, are you???

Love,
Mae-Mae

**WILNONA WILL
AND
CI-CI CAN
MAE-MIGHT...
BUT PEARLY DOES WITH EVERYONE.**

P.D. 1986

April 29, 1986

Dear Wilnona,
   I wanted to let you know that I really enjoyed this
weekend....
   These moments with you have been the best and I found
myself daydreaming of you after you left for work. I'll call
you tonight.

                                                      Love,
                                                      Pearly

P.S.
   Hope you like the rose.

May 21, 1986

Dear Mae-Mae,

    I'm sorry I haven't been in touch lately. When you hear my good news, you'll understand. I've been dating this *fine* woman I met at school. Her name is Ci-Ci Can, and she's swept me off my feet! I have to pinch myself once in a while to make sure I'm not dreaming this. After two years I finally met someone who makes me feel this way. My regret is that Pearly and my other friends don't care for her too much, but I'm hoping this will all pass. I hope you'll get to meet her soon.

                          Love, your sister,
                          Wilnona Will

June 3, 1986

Dear Wilnona,

Miz Pearly and Miss Nadine been carryin' on somethin' fierce all week. Miz Pearly found herself a new gal to play with, and that nasty ole Nadine been jealous as a hornet! I hear she been checkin' Pearly every night lookin' for hickeys, but I knows for a fact that her and this new child ain't done it yet cause they been savin' themselves for their "Big Date." And ole Nadine been gone around sayin' she wanna get back with Pearly, but Miz Pearly ain't havin' nothin' to do with her. I can't say I blame Pearly one bit, 'cause all Miss Nadine wanna do is get drunk and doped up every weekend. And I hear tell she be doin' some that crack stuff, too. And you know Miz Pearly don't want nothin' to do with that.

Anyways, like I was sayin', she been seein' this Korean gal that own a fruit stand somewhere uptown. She been seein' her every night after work but they ain't havin' the important date till Friday. Then all hell gonna break loose! I'll let you know what happens.

How you and Ci-Ci gettin' along? I can't wait to meet her, 'cause she must really be somethin'. Did you do it with her yet? Write soon.

Love, your sister,
Mae-Mae

Dear Wilnona,

You better sit down before you reads this and I knows you ain't gonna believe it, but Miz Pearly say she ain't gonna do it no more! I couldn't believe it, either, but after she done told me what all happened to her, Lord have mercy, I don't think I want to, either! Now I knows why you stay in that little apartment by yourself and not sleep with nobody for two years. After what happened to poor Miz Pearly I don't blame you one bit.

Anyways, like I tol' you in the last letter, Pearly had this big date comin' up with this oriental gal. Now I could never understand what she see in them hussies, but you know Pearly always was a little touched in the head (and after her and Miss Nadine broke up she just been a little more outta hand).

Well, Friday evenin' came and Pearly went and got herself a new suit *and new shoes*. (I knew this one was important 'cause she didn't bother to wear them high-top sneakers like she always do.) And finally she rush on over to the barbershop to get her hair cut and all slicked back.

Well, by the time Pearly got home, Miss Nadine was there. Now you know somethin' was up 'cause ole Nadine ain't been home in a long time (and I hear tell that was part a the reason they got a divorce). But Nadine sure been jealous lately.

Miz Pearly's new girlfriend been callin' her up just 'bout every night, and Miss Nadine was havin' a fit! But Pearly didn't pay her no mind and right away starts gettin' ready for this big date. While Pearly was takin' her bath, Nadine was answerin' the phone and lookin' through all the stuff that Pearly bought. Girl, she even found the present that

Miss Pearly was gonna take to Miss Ju-Lee (that Miz Pearly new girlfriend name). I never found out what it was, but you know Pearly buys her women nice things. She used to buy Miss Nadine all kinds a gold chains and earrings, diamond rings, fancy clothes, and *all* the right stuff. But you know, Nadine never did care for the stuff. (Never deserved any of it, either!)

Girl, if I wasn't hooked up with ole Bessie I'd go for Miz Pearly myself. Ha! (And I hears she real good in bed, too.)

Well, by the time Pearly got done scrubbin', cuttin' her nails, brushed her teeth with Ultra Bright, and combed her hair till you could see yourself in the shine, Miss Nadine was really mad. When Pearly walk outta the bathroom Nadine was sittin' there like some big ole nasty spider. That's when she tell Pearly that her girlfriend call and that she (Nadine) don't want her to go anyplace that night. Poor Miz Pearly. It was already eight o'clock and she only had a hour to get ready to meet this gal. And anyway, Miss Nadine had no right to do that to her, 'cause they been broken up all this time and all of a sudden she wanna be with Pearly.

But Pearly stayed and the two of them start to argue. Girl, the whole block could hear *all* their carryins on! Nine o'clock came and went and they still be screamin' and cussin'. Miz Pearly was callin' Miss Nadine a bitch and a dick lover. Miss Nadine was callin' Miz Pearly a bulldagger and a motherfucker. And the two of them be callin' each other a whole lotta nasty things! Girl, you know I had the glass to the wall! I thought Pearly was gonna let loose and hit her this time 'cause you know Miss Nadine really deserved it. But just when it was gettin' good, Nadine's family showed up at the door and the two of them shut up. Do you know they came all the way from South America just to see ole Nadine? Well, you know Pearly. She always been polite to them people and her and Miss Nadine were just the picture of the loving couple. Anyways, when Nadine see her sister they start talkin' real good 'bout how was everything in the old country, and Pearly see her chance to get away. She went right back into the bathroom and started runnin' the shower water. I guess she worked up some kinda sweat fightin' with Miss Nadine. By the time Pearly got done (again), Nadine went to the store and Pearly was rushin' to get her suit on. And then the phone rang! It was Miz Pearly new girlfriend and she was cussin' up a storm 'cause it was a quarter to eleven and Pearly ain't even left the house yet. (That Miss Ju-Lee musta been wantin' Miz Pearly somethin' fierce, 'cause she been waitin' all that time). Anyways, Pearly tried to explain what was goin' on, but Ju-Lee never did hear it 'cause she hung up before Pearly could say she'd be there in fifteen minutes. And Pearly so upset she almost tripped runnin' in them new shoes and forgot all 'bout the package she was gonna take to Ju-Lee.

Lucky for Miz Pearly that she caught a cab right away. She got there by eleven o'clock and was so happy she give the driver a extra tip for gettin' her there so fast. Girl, them New York City drivers always good in a emergency!

Anyways, Miz Pearly went inside the bar (where she was meetin' Ju-Lee) and found her drunk and carryin' on like trash with these two white butches. And that Miss Ju-Lee just ignored Pearly like she was some kinda bum.

Well, the three of them start to dance and Ju-Lee starts to rubbin' herself all up in this white girl's face and just lovin' it! Poor Pearly just stood there watchin' the whole thing till Ju-Lee and the white girls went downstairs to the bathroom. They never did come back up, so Miz Pearly went to see what was goin' on. Anyways, there was Miss Ju-Lee standin' in the bathroom with her dress all pushed up around her neck and lettin' these two butches kiss all over her and justa feelin' her titties all over the place. Well, Miz

Pearly started yellin' for Miss Ju-Lee till one a the white gals was ready to fight with her. And then that hussy Ju-Lee slap Pearly across the face and tell her she don't want nothin' to do with her ever again. Girl, I wish I coulda been a fly on the wall that night! Anyways, that Pearly can be so stupid sometimes. She went on up the stairs like nothin' happen, and come on home. And that was the end of Miz Pearly's big date.

But Lord have mercy! Wilnona, that's not all of it! The next day she never did hear from Ju-Lee and on Sunday she didn't hear from her, either, so she decided to go back to the club. I don't know if it was to look for Ju-Lee or what, but Pearly went outta the house that night lookin' wild.

Anyways, the way I heard it, Miz Pearly met these Koreans there and one of the gals took a liken to Pearly and they decides to go have some wild sex. Well, they ended up in some sleazy hotel by Washington Square, and when Miz Pearly get all her clothes off, the bitch pulls this big rubber dick outta a bag and wants to do it to Pearly! Well, you know Miz Pearly ain't havin' none a that and she throwed it out the window! Wilnona, I sure wish I coulda been there to see this big white dick come sailin' across the street! I bet some faggot justa snatched it up for himself. Well, after that it got a little rough 'cause then the gal get some handcuffs and a whip outta the bag and wanna do more stuff to Pearly. Poor Pearly damn near scared to death 'cause you know she ain't havin' none a that stuff either and they starts to fightin'. I know you don't believe this, Wilnona, but it's the Lord's honest truth. I saw Pearly when she got home. She had hickeys all over her neck and was all bruised from the bitch punchin' on her. Came home justa all shook up, but in one piece. (And I heard she had to jump outta the window with half her clothes on, too.)

Anyways, because of the Koreans, South Americans, and everybody else, Miz Pearly has had enough of women.

June 13, 1986

Dear Wilnona,

You gotta hear this one! 'Member Miz Pearly say she ain't gonna do it no more? Well, she been behavin' herself the first coupla days, but Thursday evenin' come and off she go high-steppin' all over creation. This time with a Japanese gal! Now I don't know if they did anything, but I hears she been after this gal for a long time. *Even way before Miss Nadine was even thought of.* She say this one a doctor and one a them intellectuals (whatever that mean). Miz Pearly got a habit a talkin' big words sometimes.

And that Miss Ju-Lee been callin' just about every night and damn near give Miz Pearly a heart attack. Girl, you know that hussy even showed up at Pearly's house? She be wantin' Pearly somethin' fierce!

But anyways, Miz Pearly supposed to be gettin' back with her wife, and Miss Nadine sure gonna be mad this time.

I'll write again soon, cause Miz Pearly sure go through some changes with them ladies. Tell Ci-Ci I said hi, and give my love to Missy-Mae.

Love, your sister,
Mae-Mae

P.S.
Wilnona, did you do it yet?

P.S. (again)
I hear Pearly comin' to visit you. Maybe you might want to do it with her if Ci-Ci ain't gettin any. Ha!

Dear Wilnona,

I just knows Miz Pearly carried on somethin' fierce at your house! Couldn't leave it alone, could she? I was so lonely for Pearly that I called your house lookin' for her, and Missy-Mae told me *all* 'bout the carryins on. Now tell me, Wilnona, did Miz Pearly really go to church on Sunday with the preacher's gal? Lord have mercy! You better write me real soon. 'Cause I just gotta hear bout this one. I just knows it's gonna be good. Girl, Miz Pearly is a trip.

Love, your sister,
Mae-Mae

P.S.
Wilnona, did you do it yet?
Will you ever?

A Note in Mae-Mae's Mailbox

To: Mae Might
From: Pearly Does

Yes it's true.

I took the preacher's daughter to church on Sunday. Please rest assured that we didn't do anything. However, I did carry on with *all* the other ladies!

Love, your friend,
P.D.

P.S.

Hey, Bessie, you still doing it? Ha!

June 16, 1986

Dear Wilnona,

I love you.

If you find it in your heart to get rid of Ci-Ci, please meet me this weekend. I'll send you the train ticket to New York City. I'm begging you, *please come*. You know that I'll never hurt you and will give up all those other women to be with you. I want and miss you very much and count the seconds when I'll see you again.

Call me...

My love forever,
Pearly

Dear Wilnona,

You gotta talk to Miz Pearly. She ain't listen to nobody and you the only one she gonna talk with. She gone completely crazy with this runnin' around. You know she runnin' with four different womens and still shacked up with Miss Nadine? She still goin' with the doctor (I think she like her the best outta all of them), and now she got a Sister X (she be one a them black activist from the Afrikan Women Revolutionaries), and she got another Korean gal name Kim-Chi, and a pretty little gal name Manila (she some kinda mix betweens Filipino and white, but she sure is some looker). I hopes Miss Nadine straightens out or one a them gals get Miz Pearly to settle down 'cause she been lookin' kinda ragged lately, like she sleepwalkin' or somethin'. I'm glad she goin' to visit you, but I'm sure gonna miss all the carryins on over the weekend. I just know she gonna meet somebody in Philadelphia (her name probly be Miss Friday). Ha! But you know, I always had the feelin' Miz Pearly like you somethin' special. She say if Ci-Ci don't turn your head around, that she gonna try!

I just don't know anymore 'bout her.... She tryin' to act like she twenty-one years old all over again. Member how she used to have all them nakid womens layin' up in her bed? Had a different gal for every day of the week. But I wouldn't be surprised if somebody snatches up *all* a them new gals. 'Member, that's how she lost Miss Sassy, 'cause a her runnin' around betweens New York and Philadelphia (and then some)! She could never make up her mind if she love Miss Sassy or not. Shoulda taken Sassy 'cause Nadine never do her no good, 'cept look pretty all the time.

Now if that ain't enough carryins on, Miz Pearly went and got a tattoo put on her arm. Lord have mercy, wait till you see it! Girl, I wasn't gonna tell you, but I thought I better just in case Missy-Mae there when Pearly walk in the door. It say, BORN TO EAT PUSSY in big-as-daylight letters. But Lord knows, she don't need anymore than she got already!

Wilnona, I wish I could be there when you set eyes on Miz Pearly's tattoo. That child too much for me lately! And I wish I could do somethin' 'bout ole Bessie. I just don't know…. Between Bessie and her rubber dick and Pearly with them nakid womens, my blood pressure just can't take it anymore. Write soon.

Love,
Mae-Mae

P.S.
I heard you *finally* did it!

Dear Wilnona,

That bitch Nadine really done it this time. Poor Miz Pearly finally stopped her carryins on (you know she been runnin' with five different womens) and had her house cleaned up, been cookin' her own meals, writin' up a storm, and gettin' to bed by a decent hour (by herself) every night. She cut *all* them womens loose! Yep, Miz Pearly been havin' the place to herself 'cause Nadine been shacked up with this rich white bitch. She say she in love with this one. She in love like she was in love with Miz Pearly. Ha!

Anyways, on the Fourth of July Miz Pearly went on a picnic with her friends. She ask me did I wanna go, but nasty ole Bessie had other ideas. Well, a few hours after Pearly left, in come Nadine with a coupla her friends. You know them. They be the ones she hang out with in that no-good drug place. Yeah, girl, she really be loose now that Pearly ain't keepin' a eye on things. Well, they turns up the stereo till it can't get any louder and they be carryin' on in there so bad that my walls start to vibrate. Girl, they sure was cuttin' loose that night....

They was bangin' on Miz Pearly's drums, had the dishes dirty and layin' all over the place, tore up *all* Miz Pearly's writins, and drank up all Pearly's beer. You know I saw it all! I got right up in Nadine's face and told her what a no-good hussy she was. I just knew Miz Pearly was surely gonna die when she see this mess, so's I run back home and waits for her, prayin' she don't get home too soon.

Anyways, after a coupla more hours they goes out, and 'bout midnight Miz Pearly come on home. I was still awake 'cause Bessie had to have her way with me, and you know how rambunctious she get on a Friday night. So's I goes in with Miz Pearly, and when she see the mess all she could do was sit down and cry. Then she walk from room to room justa shakin' her head and talkin' real soft to herself. It was just pitiful. Girl, it looked like the "Terminator" been all through the place! And Miz Pearly tell me to get on home, 'cause she 'bout to fall asleep. I wanted to stay the night with her, but I could hear that nasty Bessie just hollerin' for me to get my butt home, 'cause I left her sittin' in the tub playin' with that rubber dick, cussin' up a storm, waitin' for me jes so's she can torment me with her "thang." I swears, one a these days I'm gonna chop it up into little pieces! Anyways, I goes home and does my thing with Bessie (again), but couldn't sleep thinkin' 'bout poor Miz Pearly.

Round 'bout 3:30 in the mornin' I hears all this commotion and looks out the window and sees Nadine, Pearly, Nadine's girlfriend, and Nadine's brother bein' taken out by the police. I thought, *Lord have mercy! Miz Pearly really tried to kill the bitch!* Then I run out the door so fast, I almost lost my panties. Ole Bessie so horny all the time, she done tore up *all* the elastic! So's I goes on to the police station and Pearly files assault charges against Nadine's lover, 'cause the bitch try to beat up on Pearly when she be sleepin'. And not only that, the police found drugs on all of them ('cept Miz Pearly), and Nadine brother a illegal alien. Pearly the only one that ain't in any kinda trouble, so they let her go home after she fill out some kinda papers.

Anyways, there ain't been too much excitement 'round here lately. Miss Nadine move out half her stuff and only sneaks back when Pearly be at work. And Miz Pearly say she gonna be celibate for a while (whatever that mean), but I think it have somethin' to do with sex. Knowin' Miz Pearly, it probly be the latest sex position. Write soon. Give my love to Missy-Mae and Ci-Ci.

Love, your *tired* sister,
Mae-Mae

July 9, 1986

Dear Wilnona,

I hear Missy-Mae gonna visit with Miz Pearly for a spell.

Lord have mercy, Wilnona, is it true? I know how much Pearly love that girl to death and Missy-Mae just love her Miz Pearly, but you think she be able to handle all a Pearly's carryins on?

Anyways, me and Pearly gonna pick her up at the train station the day after tomorrow. Maybe Missy-Mae can make her to settle down a bit. *I hope so.*

Mae-Mae

July 15, 1986

Dear Momma,

I'm getting ready to come home and I'm glad. Please try to talk Pearly into not moving anywhere near us. If she had any kids I'm sure they would all run away. Right at this moment, I hate Pearly Does. *And she did this week,* with these nasty ladies. She's a little wild. I wish I would have let her die when she was so sick. I'm sorry, Momma, but I really do right now.

Love,
Missy-Mae

Dear Wilnona,

I justa know by now you heard from Missy-Mae. She tol' you Miz Pearly had food poisonin', didn't she, and that ole nasty Pearly be carryin' on all week and bein' sick didn't stop her none? Ha!

Well, girl, everything started out real quiet when Missy-Mae got here, but after a coupla days Miz Pearly had to let loose some her wildness and go chasin' after *all* them womens. That's when she ate that hot dog and got so sick, we thought she was gonna die for sure. (I hear she was gonna use it for some kinda reason, but the gal wouldn't let her, so Miz Pearly ate it instead).

Anyways, she laid on the livin' room floor for two days till Manila (that the gal that didn't like the hot dog) and Missy-Mae called for a ambulance to take her to the hospital. Anyways, when they gets there, Miz Pearly say she ain't lettin' no doctor touch her unless it was a woman. So they gets her a woman doctor, and Pearly tryin' to make a date with her! Lord have mercy, that Pearly be so hellified sometimes!

Anyways, they lets her go home after they gets the fever down, and her and Missy-Mae go to stay with Manila till Pearly feel better. And that's when she did her thing with Manila's nasty roommate, Noreen. (We calls her Miss Noreen Nymphette, 'cause she so horny all the time). She got a habit a walkin' around nakid all the time, and you know how Miz Pearly be about temptation. Ha! So one night when she be walkin' around bare-ass nakid, and everybody else be watchin' television, Miz Pearly got up and just disappeared. Manila think she went to the bathroom (cause Pearly be throwin' up all the time), but she ain't never come back! Wilnona, nobody never did see Miz Pearly for a coupla days! And then they call the police 'cause they thinkin' maybe she walkin' around in a awful delirium.

Anyway, one mornin' Pearly come crawlin' outta Noreen's room all covered with hickeys and stinkin' somethin' awful (like she been eatin' pussy for a coupla days!). And that nasty ole Noreen still be tryin' to pull her back into the bedroom! Wilnona, I thought I heard it *all* till now. When Missy-Mae tell me this, I just 'bout peed myself.

Anyways, Manila tell Pearly she was gonna have to leave, so her and Missy-Mae come on home and Miz Pearly been carryin' on ever since. I guess Missy-Mae be so glad to get home. Miz Pearly been treatin' her real good and givin' her anything she want, but Missy-Mae sure ain't used to all a Pearly's nakid womens. (I wish that ole nasty Bessie could eat pussy like Miz Pearly 'cause I sure am sore from that rubber dick).

Call me when you get this letter.

Love,
Mae-Mae

P.S.

Wilnona, now that you did it with Ci-Ci, are you gonna do it again?

July 23, 1986

Dear Wilnona,

What in creation is wrong with Miz Pearly???

Ever since she got back from Philadelphia she ain't been herself. Miss Kim-Chi, the doctor, Ju-Lee (she still ain't got over Miz Pearly), Sister X, and now Manila all been tryin' to get Pearly outta the house. I ask her how her visit was, and all she do is smile like some fool. Now that ain't the Miz Pearly I know. I just knows she carried on somethin' fierce over the weekend, 'cause she been plottin' and schemin' for so long over that Les Femmes affair. Lord have mercy! Did she meet up with that little gal she say she in love with? You know the one. She have a lover that took off for a spell. Wilnona, you gotta write me before I goes outta my mind. Miz Pearly keepin' awful quiet this time, and ain't even botherin' to chase after all them gals. I'm mighty tempted to go over there stark nakid and see what Pearly do. ('Cause you know she can't resist any kinda temptation!) I'm gettin' real tired a ole Bessie, and Miz Pearly might be just what the doctor ordered.

Please write soon. I'm beggin' you.

Love, your sister,
Mae-Mae

P.S.

Wilnona, are you still doin' it?
Do you like it?

P.S. (again)

I heard rumors that Nadine might be pregnant. Miz Pearly sure gonna kill her this time if it be true.

Dear Wilnona,

I knows you ain't gonna believe this, but Miss Nadine is sure 'nuff pregnant! You remember the little man she be messin' with? Well, he's the daddy and ain't takin' no responsibility for it. Now if that don't knock your socks off, she got venereal disease on top a everything else. I know Miz Pearly been to the doctor, (and, beside, her girlfriend a doctor) so I knows she didn't get it from her. Plus they ain't done anything together for a long time. Now that leaves that nasty, dirty, low-down white gal she still messin' with. I hear she got it, too. Girl, them bitches is too much! And I wouldn't be surprised if she gave the baby to Miz Pearly. Could you see Pearly bein' the daddy to some little Rasta kid with dreadlocks? Ha! Lord have mercy! What's gonna happen next??? I can't wait till summer be over so everybody can calm down. Write soon.

Love, your sister,
Mae-Mae

P.S.
   I might visit with you real soon.
   I cut Bessie's dick off.

July 28, 1986

Dear Wilnona,

I guess I ain't gonna visit you this weekend. Bessie woke up and found her dick all cut up, and damn near beat me to death. Girl, my body so beat up, it look like ten woodpeckers come peck on me. But Miz Pearly heard all the commotion and come runnin' in and save me. Good thing she strong, 'cause Bessie twenty times Miz Pearly's size! Bessie even threatened to kill her, but took off when she hear the police comin'. Anyways, Miz Pearly took me to her place, and I been here ever since. She real nice and been takin' good care of me. *I think I loves Pearly.*

The other night she come home and I decided it was time me and her got together. So's I took me a nice long bath and sprinkled on some that good perfume she like her women to wear and put on a sexy robe and them panties that untie. Now all a this time Pearly be sittin' in front a her typewriter thinkin' a some nasty story she gonna write. I know it was the wrong time to bother her, but I couldn't stand it no more. Wilnona, I been so horny for Miz Pearly, it was like dyin' and goin' to heaven just bein' by her. Anyways, I kiss Pearly on the neck, and she tells me could I go to the store and get her some cigarettes. I says, "Pearly, honey, don't you wanna come to bed?" Pearly say she busy tryin' to get the story right, and finally she look me up and down and goes on with her typin'. So's I gets dressed and goes for her nasty cigarettes. When I comes back I decides to wait for her in the bedroom. Girl, Miz Pearly finished up, took a shower, and laid down on the floor in the livin' room and left me all alone in that bed! I thought, Lord have mercy, maybe she sick or somethin'! So's I goes in the livin' room and lays down beside her and she tells me to go on back to the bedroom, 'cause she wanna be alone! Girl, she been sayin' the same thing to all them gals she be runnin' with! And last weekend Miz Pearly didn't even go out! She cook, she clean, she iron her clothes, she write, and she take naps. I think it time she see a psychiatrist. Poor Manila so upset 'cause she try to get Pearly outta the house and she sent her home cryin'. All the other times Miz Pearly would a snatched that child up and carried her off to the bedroom for a coupla days! Wilnona, do you think Pearly goin' straight? She just ain't been herself.

Anyways, like I was sayin before... I went back to the bedroom and slams the door, so Pearly know how mad I was. But she don't say a word about it. She startin' to remind me a you, when you weren't doin' it.

You still doin' it, ain't you???

I wish I was.

But I'm gonna try again with Miz Pearly. I'll take my clothes off next time. You know how she like big titties. The weekend be here soon and maybe she be ready to start her carryins on again! *I hope so.*

Write soon.

Love, your sister,
Mae-Mae

August 4, 1986

Dear Wilnona,
   I think Miz Pearly never gonna be normal.
   And I moved outta her house.
   Missy-Mae right. She *is* a little wild.

                                        Love, your sister,
                                               Mae-Mae

P.S.
   I'll write more when I gets to Miami.
   I'm goin' with Manila and Sister X.

so much she grab me and throw me down on the bed! She screw me every which way, and Lord have mercy!!! Girl, Miz Pearly know how to do it! She wanted to keep it up, but I just couldn't keep up with her. I sure wishes I had some a Pearly's energy. She make "Jane Fonda Workout" look like "Jane Fonda *Sleepin'*." (And that's just what I did.) I was so exhausted I passed out.

I don't know what time it was, but I finally woke up to all this commotion comin from the livin' room. Lord have mercy, Miz Pearly had *all* her little gals over and they was just tearin' up the place! Manila and Sister X goin' at it in the kitchen, Ju-Lee and Kim-Chi tearin' up each others' pussies, and Pearly and the doctor and this other gal watchin' porno movies on the VCR. Girl, they made the *Oriental Lesbian Fantasies* movie look like somethin' from Disneyland. Every once in a while Pearly would turn them gals over and give them a workout, and then watch the two of them screw and suck each other to death. And then Miz Pearly film the whole thing! She say she gonna show it at the erotic film festival. Wilnona, I just don't know about her. One of these days Miz Pearly gonna come to a bad end.

Anyways, by the end a the weekend Pearly had everybody cleared outta there and said she was gonna go away for a few days. Now you know I got awful suspicious, 'cause where Pearly gonna run off to, 'cept Philadelphia. (And I knows she wasn't gone there 'cause I woulda heard about it sooner.) So's I started makin' phone calls after she leave, and all her little girlfriends say she ain't nowhere to be found. Girl, we hunted for Miz Pearly all week. But she sure 'nuff disappeared this time. Poor Manila so upset, she was gonna call the police and the doctor was screamin' and carryin' on cause she think Pearly be layin' dead somewhere. All the other gals keepin' real quiet like they's scared, and even that low-down Miss Nadine got worried.

Round 'bout the next Friday evenin' Miz Pearly come

walkin' in the door like she on some kinda mission. She wearin' a white suit and lookin like she ain't for real. Right away Manila start screamin' that Pearly's ghost come back to haunt us. But she real all right, cause the doctor check her out. When we all got back to our senses, Pearly tell everybody to sit down 'cause she got somethin important to tell us. So's we all sits down, and that's when Pearly tell us she gonna get married. Girl, we started laughin so hard, (cause we all thought it was a joke), that I almost peed myself! Ha! But Miz Pearly was sure 'nuff serious. She get real mad and tell all a us to get outta her house, 'cause she in love with this gal and nobody gonna talk her outta it. Lord have mercy, Wilnona, did you know anything about this? I didn't know Pearly been seein' anybody, other than them gals she usually be messin' with. Where she ever get the time to find anybody else? None a us ever laid eyes on this child! Anyways, Pearly tell us that this the one gal she been wantin' all along, but we can all still be friends. And that's when she tell us we all gotta act real proper round her new woman! Girl, if looks could kill, Pearly Does would be dead six times over. I just knows I'm gonna hate this new child. That Miz Pearly sure did lose her mind after her and Miss Nadine broke up.

Anyways, we still in Miami. I think I'm gonna go home soon and hook up with Sister X. She real nice. And Bessie had a nervous breakdown and been in the hospital ever since I chopped up her rubber dick, so's I don't think she gonna be able to cause any trouble for a long time.

I'll write again when I calms down.

Love, your sister,
Mae-Mae

P.S.
Are you goin' to Pearly's weddin'?

August 12, 1986

Dear Wilnona,

Before you read this, you better sit down.

It may come as a shock to you, but I'm getting married again. Her name is Iola, and she's a wonderful, warm, sensitive, and beautiful woman. We've been secretly seeing each other all these months to avoid gossip and I didn't want her to hear about my lascivious reputation. I'm now madly in love with her and have stopped all my running around. Anyway, I guess you know all about this, and about the orgy (because Mae-Mae can never keep her mouth shut). Do you know she went to Miami with *all* of my ex's? All I want now is for everybody to like Iola and hope you all forgive me (soon). I'm anxious for you to meet her. She's such a good woman. Give my love to Missy-Mae.

Love,
Pearly

P.S.

When the part comes for the minister to ask why Iola and I shouldn't be united, please make sure everybody keeps their mouths *shut*. Thanks.

Dear Wilnona,

You better sit down before you reads this, cause here we go again!

You ain't gonna believe this, but Bessie gettin' married. And girl, here's the good part...it ain't to no woman, either.

Miz Pearly call and tell me the other night. We's all friends again, and everybody goin' to Pearly and Iola's weddin'. Just couldn't stay mad with her, 'cause Pearly been so nice with me. Have you met Iola yet? I'm just dyin' to meet her. Me and Sister X gonna come home next week.

Anyways, Bessie met this man in the hospital. She still there, and plannin' to have the weddin' and reception in the hospital cafeteria. Can you beat that? All this time she torment me with that rubber dick, and now she got the "real thang" from this man! Lord have mercy, Miz Pearly say he white, too. And none a us goin' to Bessie's weddin' 'cause we didn't get a invite. The only reason Pearly know is cause she used to go out with one a the nurses. I even heard ole Bessie so horny, that one night she even did it in a closet! Yeah, girl, one a the night nurses come 'round to check on the patients and found Bessie and Alvin (that her boyfriend name) missin'. There was just no way they could climb outta the windows ('cause they got bars on them), and all the doors goin' outside are locked up tight. So that mean they still gotta be somewhere inside the hospital. Well, the security guards start searchin' all over the place and they finds Bessie in a broom closet. And there she was, just a suckin' away, till there ain't no tomorrow, on this man's dick! Wilnona, when Pearly tell me this, I thought I was gonna die laughin'! And Bessie say when she get out, she gonna teach Alvin how to eat pussy.

Lord have mercy, Wilnona! Between Miz Pearly and Bessie and everybody else, I sure don't need any more excitement in my life. Either my blood pressure won't take it, or I'll be in the nuthouse with crazy Bessie.

Manila went back to New York a coupla days ago and wants to be a sister in one a them convents. I guess she be joinin' Bessie *real soon*.

Ju-Lee and Kim-Chi goin' back to Korea, and the doctor goin' back to bein' celibate. (That's how she was before she met up with Pearly.) And I found out it do have somethin' to do with sex, but it just mean you don't have any! Anyways, me and Sister X real happy and might be settlin' down, too (if we survive this summer)! Lord have mercy, it sure been fun, though. I'm gonna miss all the carryins on now that Pearly gonna settle down and Bessie crazy now.

How you and Ci-Ci gettin' along? I guess you be settlin' down, too, and then there won't be no more excitement 'cept if Missy-Mae get pregnant or somethin'. I just can't wait till I gets home so's I can see this Iola child. I'll call you soon.

Love,
Mae-Mae

August 25, 1986

To Pearly Does:
    Stay away from Iola if you want to live.
    I know where you hang out and will come looking for you.

                      Signed,
               The Cat Woman

August 27, 1986

Dear Wilnona,

I been just beside myself with grief. I can't sleep or eat anymore just knowin' Miz Pearly be dead. At first none a us wanted to believe it (even Nadine), but the police report say the blood in the alley sure 'nuff match up with poor Pearly. And they even found two used bullets layin' there alongside the spot where she been shot. But Lord have mercy, where Miz Pearly's body? And now the Cat Woman took off and poor Iola can't be found. That poor gal so upset, she probably gone off and done somethin' awful, 'cause she say she can't live without her true love Pearly.

I knows I always said that Pearly would come to a bad end ('cause a her messin' with too many womens), but I never thought she be shot down outside one a them lesbian bars. It's so hard to believe.

Me and Sister X comin' to stay with you 'cause I can't stand livin' next to Pearly's empty apartment.

Your sorrowful sister,
Mae-Mae

Dear Wilnona,
    Have you heard anything from Pearly yet?
    I can't believe she's dead somewhere and just know it was her that Lucy saw sleepin' on the bench at the Trenton, New Jersey, train station. And not only that, I had a dream that Pearly was hidin' out till Iola and the Cat Woman left town. I still ain't sure what it mean, but it sure to mean a lot. If Pearly really be dead I think her ghost would come and haunt us (especially Nadine), 'cause you know Miz Pearly would do somethin' like that.
    Call me soon. I can't take it no more and gotta know what you found out.

Love,
Mae-Mae

Dear Wilnona,

I just can't believe what Lucy told me over the phone last night. What gone wrong with Miz Pearly? First she cut *all* them nakid womens loose and then she wanna marry that Iola gal, and then her and the Cat Woman have a make-pretend gunfight and make everybody think she dead somewhere, and then she wanna be sleepin' in the train station, and now she wanna run outta the country! Lord have mercy, Wilnona, I think she gonna be joinin' Bessie before crazy Manila do. And if she go in the nuthouse there's no tellin' what Miz Pearly be doin'. I just knows she be carryin' on all over again! I'm sure glad I'm with Sister X now, but wish you and Pearly coulda settled down. Maybe when she get back from where she goin'??? ('Cause it don't look like you and Ci-Ci gonna be doin' it for too much longer.)

Well, sis, I don't know what else to say. I'll write again when I calms down. This will sure 'nuff be over again soon.

Love, your confused sister,
Mae-Mae

My dear sister Mae-Mae,

I apologize for not being in touch most of the summer. As you know, I met this fine thang named Ci-Ci. Well, we had seen each other at school and at the social dances for over a year and by the beginning of May we *finally* hit it off! We started dating as much as our schedules would allow. It was wonderful. Ci-Ci absolutely "ravished" me, and most of all, we could talk, in and out of the bedroom. We spent so many quiet and special times together. I enjoyed them so very much and began to think maybe this was my "light at the end of the tunnel." I would go to her house every Friday after work (while Missy-Mae was away at camp), and leave there Monday morning for work. It was great and I was looking forward to our future together. However, my bubble was busted and I was brought down to earth.

While I was on vacation last week, Ci-Ci had one of her "headaches" and wished not to be bothered by anyone. We did not spend any time together or even talk on the phone. By the beginning of this week she called to apologize for being so abrupt the last time we spoke and said she felt we needed to talk. We decided I would go to see her on Friday. Well, any other time when Ci-Ci and I were going to spend time together I would get a lump in my stomach and a big grin on my face. This time I got very nervous. I realized then that I had felt this way during most of my vacation. I spent all of last week trying to keep busy and talking with my friend Lucy. We discussed the vibes I had been feeling about Ci-Ci, the relationship, and where it was going. I even went so far as to write Ci-Ci a letter, telling her I knew she was going to let me go. Lucy told me I was "jumping the gun" and that Ci-Ci was *not* thinking of breaking up with me. I ended up not sending the letter, but even so, the lost and empty feelings did not go away.

Well, my dear sister, Lucy was so wrong, and I was so right. On Friday, Ci-Ci told me it was nice, she enjoyed what we had and would always treasure the relationship. However, it was all over between us. Hey! You know me... I gave it my best "OK, fine" attitude, said I understood, I had expected it, held back the tears, gathered myself, and left. *I was crushed.* I cried all the way home on the bus, and cried myself to sleep.

Today I got up and went out with one of my friends (to keep myself from crying all day around the house). So I thought while I had a little composure about myself I would write you a letter and let you know I will not be answering the phone, or seeing people for a little while. You know I will withdraw into my shell now. It hurts! So take care, be good, tell Pearly I said hi, and please give me some time to myself while I try to regroup.

Love, your sister,
Wilnona Will

P.S.
Well, Wilnona *Won't*, for a long time to come.

September 8, 1986

My dearest love Wilnona,

    I can't begin to tell you how sorry I was to hear that you and Ci-Ci broke up. I also realize you need your space now, and so I'll respect your wishes. I'm only glad Missy-Mae is there with you, so you won't be lonely. Just remember in your solitude that I care for you deeply and always will.

    As for what happened between me and Iola? I realized I never loved her, and that it was you I have always loved. The fake gunfight with the Cat Woman worked well and she was more than happy to have Iola back. They belong together just as you and I belong together.

    And as for me? I'm going to the Philippines to join the revolutionaries. I'll write to you whenever I can and will try to return to the States by next summer. Just remember I will be back for you. Maybe then you'll be able to give *my love* a try. Until then, my thoughts and spirit are with you.

Love forever,
Pearly

P.S.

    Give my love to Missy-Mae. She has known all along about my plans, so please thank her for keeping "our secret."

Dear Wilnona,

I guess you know by now that Miz Pearly left for the Philippines yesterday. She probly gonna join up with them revolutionaries and get thrown outta the country. Ha! She say she just goin' there to write, but we'll just see about that. I just know she gonna meet up with some little gal where she goin', but you know and I know that it ain't never gonna last long. And I never did understand what happened between her and that Iola child. Ain't that somethin'? It sure been some crazy summer.

I'm awful sorry to hear 'bout you and Ci-Ci breakin' up, and now I'm glad I never got to meet her. Miz Pearly and everybody else never did like her too much anyways. Besides, I think you and Pearly gonna meet up again one a these days and settle down. I just knows you gonna miss her somethin' fierce, but you be glad to be gettin' back to school and havin' Missy-Mae home. I'm gonna be studyin', too, 'cause Sister X want me to learn spellin' and readin'. Sister X so smart. I been goin' to meetins with her, and they got these classes at night for folks that wanna learn all kinds of stuff. And we startin' a support group for Lesbian Muslims and havin' our first meetin' tonight. Next week Sister X gonna give a workshop at Medgar Evers College in Brooklyn.

Well, I guess I'm not gonna hear from you for a while, and maybe not till next summer when and if Miz Pearly get back. It be time by then to take off them socks and long underwear, if you know what I mean...

Give my love to Missy-Mae and tell all the gang I said hi.

Love and Solidarity,
Your Sister,
Mae-Mae X

P.S.

Wilnona, if you need anything call me collect ('cause I just won the Lotto)!

And just remember that me and all your friends care 'bout you and think Ci-Ci is a jerk.

P.S. (again)

Do you think you wanna go on the Lesbian Love Boat Cruise to Bermuda in July that Miss Frank's organization is havin'? It sure be nice. Me and Sister X gonna be goin' and we'll pay for your ticket. Maybe Miz Pearly go, too. Ha!

ABOUT *the* AUTHOR

Chea Villanueva is a forty-two-year-old butch of Filipino-Irish ancestry and believes this combination of strong cultures has helped make her what she is today. Much of her writing is based on people, places, and situations she has encountered in her own life.

She is the author of *Girlfriends*, *The Chinagirls*, and *The Things I Never Told You* (poetry). Her fiction and poems have also appeared in *The Persistent Desire*, *The Body of Love*, *Outrage*, *The Poetry of Sex*, *Common Lives/Lesbian Lives*, *Making Waves*, *Riding Desire*, *Feminary*, *Ang Katipunan* (Union of Democratic Filipinos), *The South Street Star*, *Matrix*, and *Big Apple Dyke News*.

An essay on her life and work appears in *Contemporary Lesbian Writers of the United States*.